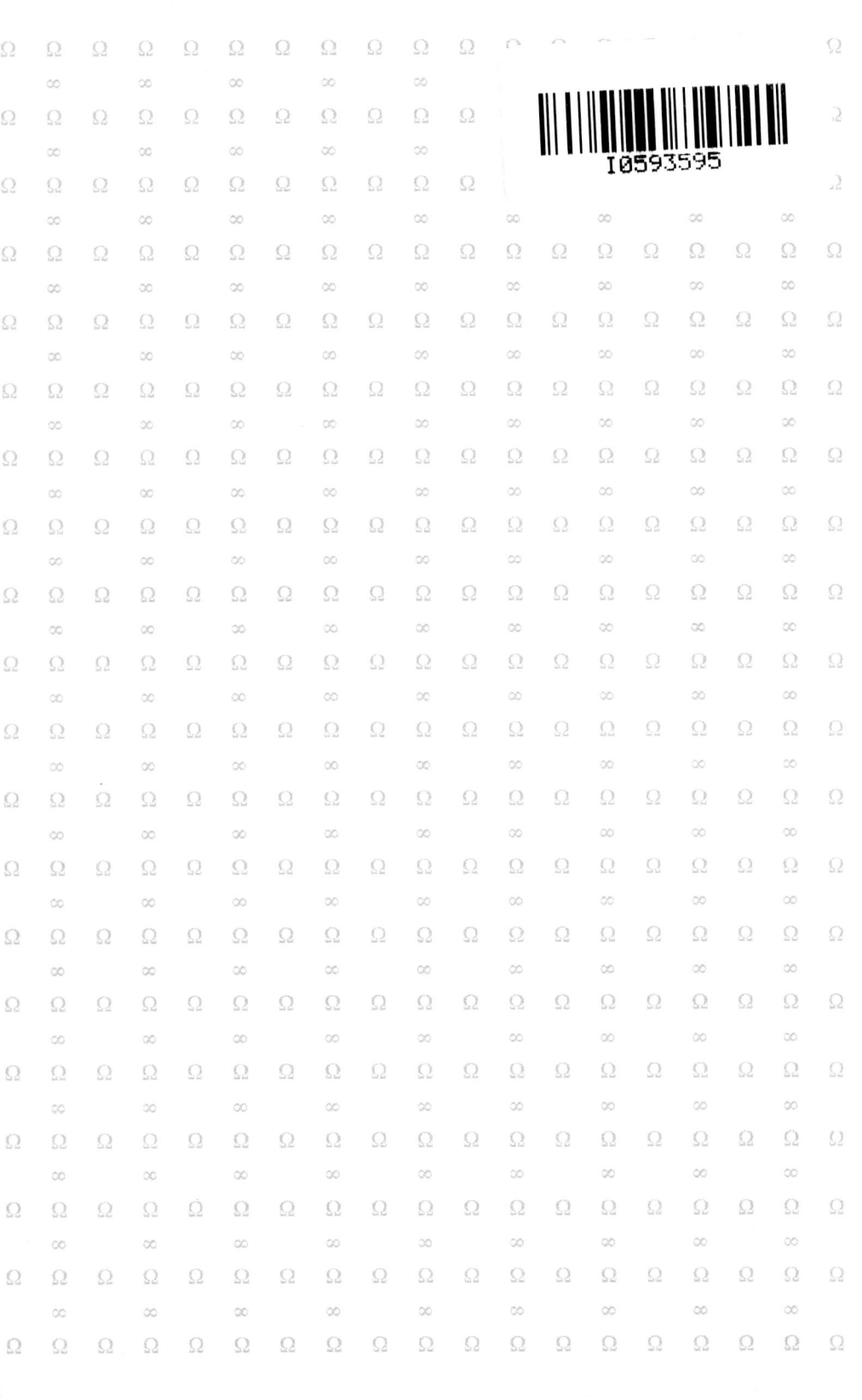

I0593595

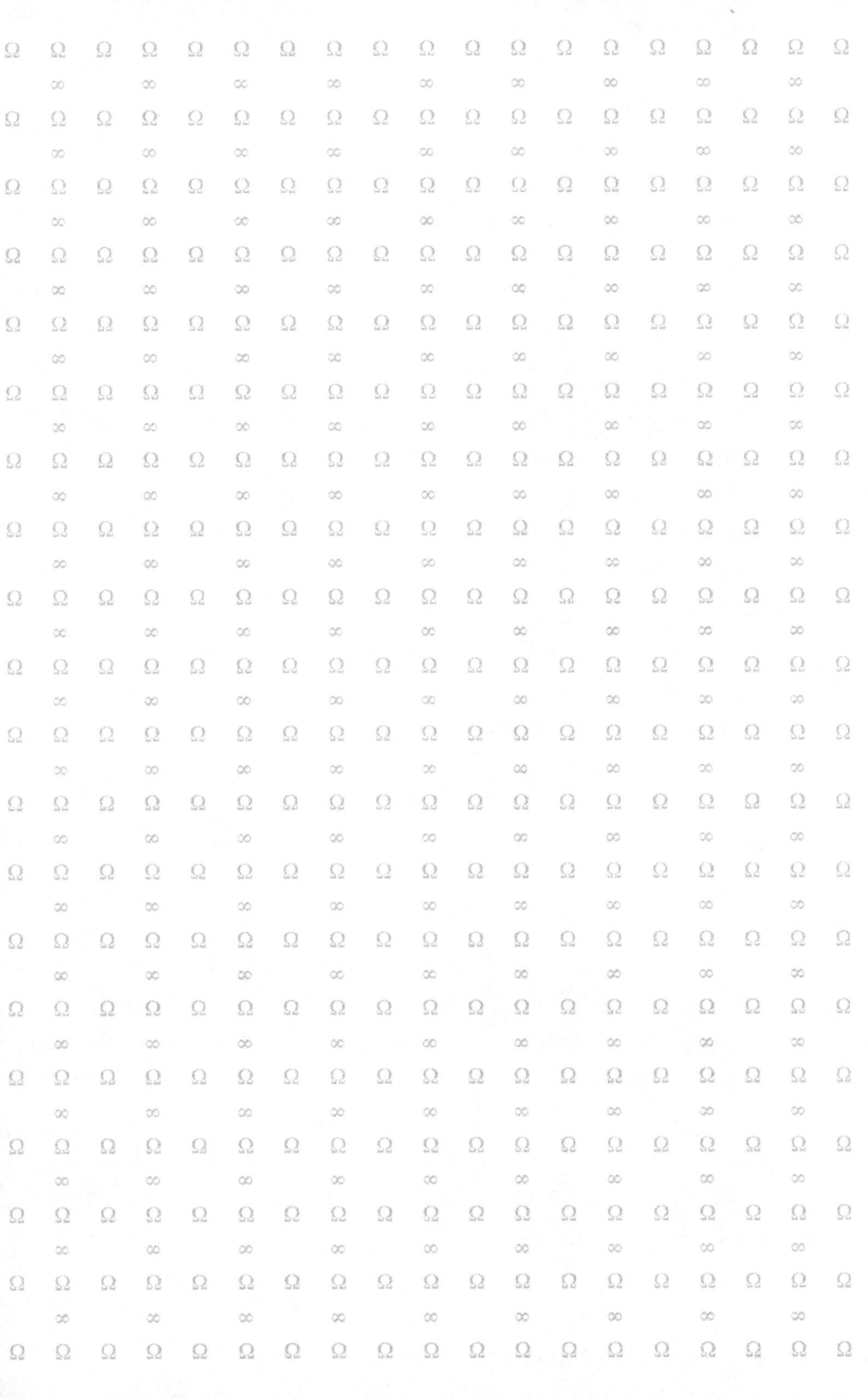

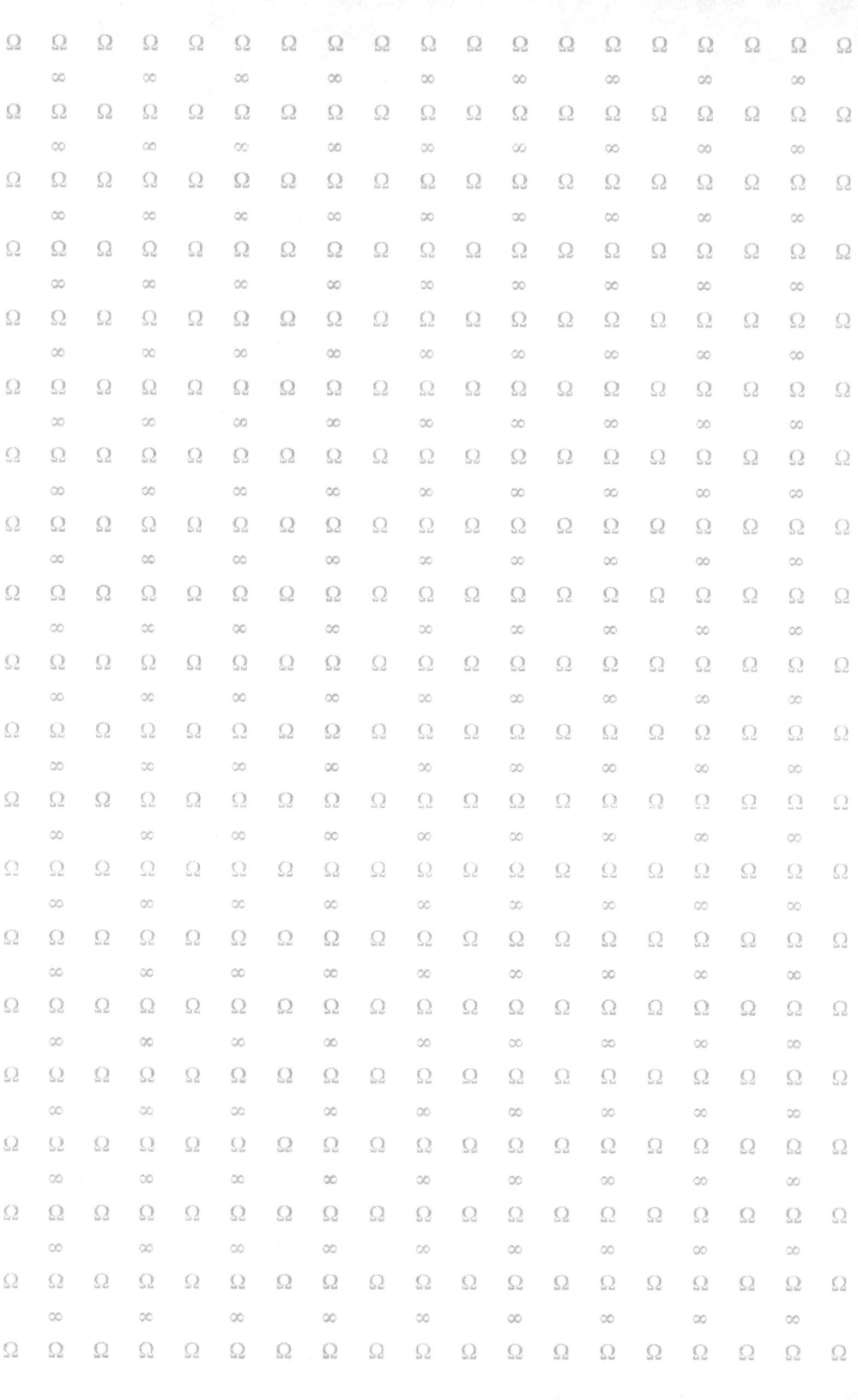

Smothered

Graeme Sparkes

in case of emergency press

We are proud to acknowledge the Traditional Owners of
country throughout Australia.
We pay our respects to their Elders.
We support recognition, reconciliation, and reparation.

Smothered

Graeme Sparkes

in case of emergency press
http://www.icoe.com.au
Travancore, Victoria
Australia

Published by **in case of emergency press** 2023

ISBN 978-0-6456382-3-3

Cover and Title Page painting: **Jill Bolitho**
Photograph of painting: **Vincent Galante**

Dedication

To those who never bonded

Acknowledgements

I'd like to thank **Clémence Overall** for her early reading of *Smothered* and her encouragement. Thanks also to my editor, **Howard Firkin**, for his hard work and patience.

Thanks also to my partner, **Sonia**, for her forbearance.

1

It wasn't my idea to participate in a bedside vigil for my father. My mother wanted me there. Soon after she had learnt of his prognosis she phoned and begged me to return to the family home.

"Despite what you think, Alan," she said, anticipating my resistance. "Tosh has always loved you."

She would have heard my acid laugh but refrained from her usual dudgeon, knowing it would make her task harder. "Do the decent thing, darling, and don't let him down."

There was a pause while she searched for some remembrance to persuade me. "You know, when you were a baby, Tosh was so delighted he had a son he used to throw you way up in the air."

"Did he bother to catch me?"

"Of course he did."

"Why of course?"

"He loved you, that's why," she repeated. "But you were that scared you used to scream every time he did it. Most boys would squeal, they'd enjoy it so much, but not you."

"Perhaps, even as a baby, I didn't trust him."

"Face it, Al, you were a scaredy cat, but he was over the moon. A son! When Pam was born first, he was that upset it was like he had the PND, not me. It's true, don't laugh. I can hear you sneering, Alan. Tosh just wanted a boy, that's all. A son to share his dreams with. Can I be frank with you? I know you don't like criticism but I feel I've got to say this. You let him down. Big time. I want you to keep that in mind as he—as his health deteriorates."

She hesitated, upset by her allusion to his dying.

I remained silent.

"Al? Are you still there?"

I grunted, trying my hardest to be civil.

"Can't you say something?"

"You've always taken his side."

"I'm not saying it was all your fault. At times he was a bit rough on you. He'd admit that now, I'm sure. So it's not too late to make amends. You know that, don't you, love? I do hope you'll be there for him. I think you owe him that much."

I begged to differ. In my humble opinion, I owed him nothing. His attempts to make me in his own image had been no more successful than the Almighty. But I could see the old dear needed my support, if only to prepare for her life without him.

Raymond McIntosh—Tosh—was dying. Everyone called him Tosh, and so did I once I discovered it could mean *nonsense*. Sometimes I altered it to Tosher: *the one who searches for valuables in drains and sewers.*

2

My cries as he threw me in the air should have warned him that his plans for me were unlikely to succeed. But he missed the early signs, blinded by certainty. I don't remember him tossing me aloft, but if what my mother claimed is true, then undoubtedly it had a negative impact on my early years.

One of my earliest memories of him involved a massive toy truck, which loomed over me when I was seated on the floor, just out of nappies, although I'd been in nappies far longer than the average infant for reasons I don't wish to go into, although you might speculate it had something to do with my upbringing. Tosh gave me the truck as a present for my fourth birthday, but apparently I didn't show enough enthusiasm or gratitude. He took me outside and instructed me to load it with dirt. I did once or twice but without much enthusiasm, without mimicking the noises of heavy machinery he expected from a bona fide boy. Pam recently told me I liked her toys better, and she had been generous enough to let me play with them.

He would have warned me about playing with dolls, squatted before me with big hands gripping my skinny arms, staring at my face, as if searching—for what? Some sign of masculinity? I doubt he found anything to reassure him. His eyes would have been anxious—he had not yet given up on me—their paradoxical stare, simultaneously beseeching and hostile. Dry pale eyes that had never cried. No eyelashes to speak of. Red rims as flaky as the painted guttering around our house. "If I ever see you playing with your sister's things," he once warned thoughtfully, when I was a bit older and he caught me in Pam's room, not looking at dolls but books, "I'll kick your arse so hard you won't be able to sit down for a month." His thin lips had scabs. His dull, greasy hair, always had a flurry of dandruff. A thick fringe, falling as far as his eyebrows, singed from careless attempts to light his cigarettes on our gas stove, was in homage to his favourite musicians, The Rolling Stones.

I'll have to take my mother's word for it: he doted on me when I was an infant. He believed in my potential. But I gave him no reason for optimism. I was a sickly child—asthmatic, prone to catch colds, underweight thanks to a fastidious palate, jaundiced at times and easily bruised. Yet he had faith. Nothing could shake his belief that his genetic contribution could result in anything other than a robust manifestation of masculinity. It would just take time. He would have to be patient. (Later, rather than abandon that assumption, he would agree with me to question the source of my genetic material.)

I don't remember much more about him from my first few years because he *was* patient. Nothing he did disturbed me enough to leave further indelible marks on my infant psyche. Except one thing. I learned he was a butcher. My mother took me along with Pam to see him at work one day. Maybe she took us a few times. I remember him dressed in a white apron that was covered in blood. He slammed a cleaver into a slab of meat and said, "This is what happens to little boys if they don't listen to their dads." He burst into laughter along with everyone else in the shop, except Pam, who started to cry, which set me crying too. It ruined his fun, as now his wimpy son was embarrassing him.

And it affected my appetite for meat.

My mother in those days was more protective of me. She pleaded with him to go easy on me. I was still young. There was plenty of time for me to develop. She suggested encouraging intellectual pursuits, but apart from reading and learning the times table, she was at a loss to suggest anything that would interest me. "He's got a good head on him, Tosh," she said and made a joke about not knowing where I got my brains from. "He might go to university one day and make us all proud."

Although I hadn't a clue what university was, I appreciated my mother's support and protection. She fussed over me, always made sure I was clean and tidy and that I brushed my teeth. She taught me how to tie my own shoelaces. She warned me about talking to strangers, although she had little to worry about on that account; I hardly talked to members of my own family, much less anyone else. Sometimes she watched kids' TV shows with me. And she tucked me into bed each night, even after I grew older and no longer appreciated her maternal attention. In return I did small chores, like emptying the kitchen tidy, or I'd clean her shoes, as well as my own, and when I was big enough I'd help her to dry the dishes. That was before Tosh bought her a dishwasher. She used to ruffle my hair and say, "Good boy. I reckon you'll look after me when I get old and grey."

When she was younger my mother was what most men would call attractive. According to photos I've seen, she had blond hair and was invariably dressed in clothes that accentuated her figure. She stood with her parents, her girlfriends, or with Tosh who seemed a bit stunned, as if he couldn't believe his luck. But he was good-looking too, already with a thick fringe and pouting lips. And I got the impression the attraction was purely physical, for both of them. If there was anything cerebral going on between them, I couldn't detect any evidence of it as I was growing up. They seemed to belong to totally different tribes—hers exclusively female, his exclusively male—which came together when circumstances required it, weddings, funerals, birthdays, meals, sex, and the like, but otherwise they had little in common. I think her biggest disappointment was Tosh's reluctance to dance. He completely lacked a sense of rhythm, ironic given his obsession with the Rolling Stones. She could do the swing, the jitterbug, rock'n'roll, and the twist, as well as the unsophisticated jerking around that passed as dancing when they were young. She teasingly called him "Lurch".

My sister, Pam, was also supportive most of the time. I was her only sibling, which seemed to matter a lot to her. If we had other brothers or sisters, I think her attention would have been less focused on me. But I was the only one with whom she could share her wisdom, gained in the two years more she had spent on this earth than I had, like how the anatomy of girls and boys differed, and how to wipe my bum properly after a poo, for which I was naively grateful. I suspect she realised she was the lucky one, not having to face the demands our father put upon me just because I was a boy. Her gratitude manifest in small acts of generosity, like sharing her toys and picture books, and letting me watch her pee behind the garden shed.

I don't want to give the impression that my younger years were completely woebegone and damaging. I felt very close to my mother and sister. The time I spent with them has given me some fond memories. We went to the zoo, to Luna Park and to the movies together. Often they took me to shopping centres, and we wandered around looking at clothes and shoes and kitchenware. I was allowed to play in the indoor adventure playgrounds, although I mainly stood back and watched what the other kids were doing. And before we went home, we would consume donuts and milk shakes in the food court with dozens of cheerful families.

But I won't dwell on my mother and sister; my concern is with my father. I reached five or six before he began to make further demands on me. I remember it began with the sea. He took me to the beach, an ocean beach somewhere along the Surf Coast, not a tame stretch of Port Phillip Bay. My mother and sister must have been there, one of our brief summer holidays. It was the unyielding waves, the way they sucked and gouged the sand, that I dreaded the most. They loomed above me as they approached the shore, where I stood resisting Tosh's cajoling. He was in the sea, up to his thighs, sometimes up to his chest, his arms outstretched, hands waving in an impatient gesture for me to join him. Was he mad? Did he want me to drown? On terra firma I barely came up to his chest. He rushed ashore and grabbed me, dragged me into the surf, ignored my screams and asthmatic gasps, shouting something about *only one way to learn*, releasing me, surrendering me to the mercy of the waves, which seized me, toyed with me, forced me down and around, invaded my mouth, thrust me up, and delivered me onto the indifferent beach, where I tried to howl but vomited brine. I remember his laugh and declaration. "That was fun!"

The fun was his. Always was. Except at the end.

I should have mentioned Cassius. Tosh brought home a dog. A Staffordshire Terrier. It frightened me at first even though it was a puppy. It had teeth that wanted to latch onto something—anything—and not let go. It grabbed a sleeve of my bunny hug jacket and shook me around. I looked at Tosh, hoping he would intervene, but he didn't. He laughed. "It's just mucking around," he said. "Shake him back. He'll like that."

It did. My effort was feeble, partly because I wasn't as strong as the puppy, partly because I was scared. It responded with a menacing growl and bared its teeth, still holding my sleeve. I cried out, "It's going to bite!"

"Don't be a wuss," he counselled. "It's only a pup, for God's sake. Growl at him. Tell him to let go. You've got to be the boss, remember."

I tried.

"No, no. Use a deep voice. Like this." He snarled instructions at it, even slapped its muzzle until it cowed away. He put it on a leash and said, "Come on, we'll take him to the park."

Outside he handed me the leash and began to trot away from us, calling Cassius, who sprang after him. It was only a pup but I was a weak child. Feisty, enthusiastic, impulsive (all traits I lacked), it hauled me off my feet and dragged me a metre or so along the footpath, skinning my palms and knees before I let go. Tosh saw it happen and heard me bawling. His hands wavered between fists and flared palms of frustration. His eyes rolled heavenward. "Can't you do anything?" he said, despairing, as he lifted me to my feet, glanced at the damage, and nudged me to go home. "Get your mother to put something on them knees. I'll walk Cassius by myself."

To my consternation he didn't give up on me. He made me lead Cassius again the next day, this time without running ahead. He had called the dog Cassius after his favourite boxer, better known as Muhammad Ali, except Tosh didn't like Muslim names, or, for that matter, Muslims in general, so he christened it Cassius, after rejecting Chum, the name I wanted. He walked beside me, ready to grab the leash if Cassius reacted impulsively to other temptations.

The park was at the end of our street. Tosh would sometimes let Cassius off the leash to socialise with other dogs. It was a big park with eucalypts, picnic tables, timber benches and a children's playground. There were also young mothers he liked to engage in conversation. I preferred the swings until one day Tosh got behind me and began to push. Each thrust took me higher, past the horizontal, heading for the perpendicular, until I screamed and he relented under the disapproving gaze of other park users. "Must you always draw attention to yourself?" he muttered, glancing at a couple of mothers nearby.

We went to the park on days when he wasn't working. He taught me how to throw the ball for Cassius, which I quite liked, and he tried to get me to climb on the monkey bars, which I resisted. "Can't I keep playing with Cashews?"

"For Christ's sake, it's Cassius." He grabbed my arm and began to drag me. "Cashews are nuts."

I tried a feeble joke. "He's got nuts, look."

He glanced at me surprised, pleased, hearing me utter a blokey riposte. "Come on then," he said, hopeful. "I loved climbing these things when I was your age. You won't fall off, I promise, not unless you're a dickhead."

He lifted me to the bars and I moved from one to the next, tentatively, terrified of falling, unconvinced he would catch me before I hit the ground. I reached the other end, wheezing, but without incident and felt triumphant. He lifted me from the monkey bars, hugged and almost kissed me. "That's my boy!" He turned to the nearest mother. "Did you see my kid?" he asked. "Ray, by the way. I live just near here." He grinned at her and she grinned back. For a while he and I were the best of pals.

The next few times we went to the park he told me to play with Cassius while he chatted to the mother, who returned with a pram each day. On one occasion he asked me to stay in the park and he went off somewhere with her, and came back alone an hour or so later, smiling, looking happier than I had ever seen him and instructing me not to tell *mummy* that he left me alone or he would instruct Cassius to bite me.

"He won't do that," I whimpered.

"He'll do what I tell him to. And you bloody well will too."

I was too young to understand what he was up to or why he didn't want my mother to know, but she had secret friends too. I heard her talking on the phone to one, when Tosh was at work. She laughed and talked quickly and moaned in a pleasant way. "Stop it, Don, stop," she trilled. "Not on the phone." As I watched, she pressed her hand into her lap, until she noticed me and abruptly ended the call. I only remember this because she told me she had been talking to Donald Duck and he had rung up to ask her to show me his latest cartoon, and that was what we did; we watched cartoons together. And afterwards she entertained me with her attempts to mimic Daffy Duck's voice and waddle, which was so ridiculous I laughed until the pain had me gasping, and she raced to find my reliever puffer.

But I got to meet Don by accident at a shopping centre, and he was no duck. He swooped on Mum, more like a raptor, put his arm around her waist, and kissed her cheek. Alarmed, she glanced at me and Pam, and tried to escape his embrace.

"Kids, this is Mary's husband, being cheeky. You know Mary—Mrs Evans?"

"Don," he said, extending his hand to greet me. "Pleased to meet you, little man."

I asked, "Are you the Don that rings Mum?"

He looked at her and chuckled. "Smart fella."

She laughed shrilly and denied it with such force she startled me.

Then making the occasion more memorable, Don led us to an ice cream parlour and bought us triple-scoop cones. Halfway through mine, it toppled into my lap and my mother had to take me into the Ladies to clean me up, an experience that has kept Don (Duck) in my memory all these years, although I never saw him again.

Tosh asked me to help him build a kennel, as a reward for my obedience. It was more of an observational role than participatory. He sat me on a crate in his workshop and gave me ear muffs to deaden the sound of his power tools.

I watched him cut timber on his saw bench, his forehead furrowed and his lips pursed in concentration. He stared, unflinching, at the timber he was cutting. Oils and paints in containers gave the shed a pungent smell, which I liked. The lights were bright and honest. With my mother, sister and Cassius kept away, I felt privileged.

He screwed a frame together, nailed some weatherboards to it and added a gabled roof. To finish, he showed me a copper plate etched with *Cassius*. He drilled a couple of holes, held the plate in place, and handed me a screwdriver. "Your turn, little man." After a couple of failed attempts, with his patience unexpectedly enduring, I managed to complete the task. "We'll make a carpenter of you yet," he declared and grinned.

Perhaps that placated him.

3

He didn't trouble me again for a few years. He ignored me, and I assumed that was the normal thing fathers did. I was happy to spend my time at home with my mother and sister.

He was there, of course, starting his own business apparently, relinquishing his part-time job as a butcher to run a fast-food chicken joint, to be his own boss as he often boasted, although to the rest of us, particularly towards the end of his life, he seemed like its slave. I was starting school, so there were more important matters on my mind than his new enterprise.

Making friends was one of them. I remember the dread I felt on my first day at school, my mother abandoning me in a classroom where there were other kids my age, some of them crying, some of them as frightened as me, some of them running around, shouting and laughing, already letting the rest of us know who would be running the show. The timid ones huddled together, which is how I met Simon, who by the end of the day was my best friend. We sat together at a table and drew our homes on butcher paper with crayons. There was Mum next to the house, waving towards the viewer, Pam playing with Cassius, and Tosh spraying water over his car, while Simon's house was tiny, much smaller than his mother, who stood with a down-turned mouth next to an empty pram. There were no brothers or sisters or a father around. The teacher, whose name escapes me, a woman about my mother's age but more fearsome-looking, told us our pictures were beautiful. We were allowed to stick them on the wall. Simon and I went to recess feeling less tense. I wanted to hold his hand but he pulled away and said boys didn't do that, there were no other boys doing it, and the teacher would smack us. So, I occupied my hands with a bucket and spade in the sandpit.

Much of my first year at school was fun, better than home, and I began to look forward to the years ahead, especially with my friend Simon by my side. We would sit together through the next few grades.

Early on in my education I was diagnosed with myopia. I needed glasses, which helped explain my physical awkwardness but dismayed Tosh. I remember him saying, "Wouldn't you know it, he's a four eyes!"

I didn't need glasses for books, just for the whiteboard and to see into the distance. Learning quickly to please the teacher, I could read before most others in our class. Simon was slower. I tried to help him but he was angry and said books were rubbish and boring. He preferred TV. He allowed me to come to his place to watch it with him. He lived a couple of streets from our place. My mother gave me permission.

The first time I went there his mother had something wrong with one of her eyes, which was swollen and bloody and looked ready to fall out of its socket. Some of her teeth were missing. Simon told me his father had knocked her around and disappeared. And if he came home his mother would ring the police. We watched cartoons so we didn't have to think about his return. Simon's mother gave us cordial.

Tosh sometimes hit my mother, although he never maimed her. He was careful how he hit her. There were bruises but they were easily concealed beneath clothes. I can't remember exactly why he used to hit her, but he didn't like it when she went out by herself. When she came home, he would be in a dark mood. They would argue. He would call her a "filthy liar", she would deny whatever it was he'd accused her of, he would repeat it, only louder, and their arguments would escalate until he hit her. I watched sometimes from behind an armchair or the door and would run away when the hitting and screaming started. I didn't understand until I was much older that he suspected her of behaving as he did.

One day when I met up with Simon at our favourite spot near the creek in our neighbourhood, he punched me in the mouth. I felt my lip split and tasted blood. I began to moan and snivel. "What was that for?"

He shrugged and put his hands in the pocket of his shorts. "Practising," he said.

We were by ourselves. Nobody else saw him hit me. He walked off and threw stones at a bird pecking the ground on the other side of the creek.

Our friendship suffered. I didn't want to be with him anymore. But I didn't have another friend. So, I hung around. I remember he came to the football with me once to watch Tosh play. I don't recall what competition it was but probably a minor league. The game wasn't at an important stadium because cars could be parked around the boundary. My mother drove us there. She and my sister stayed in the car while Simon and I got out to be as close to the action as we could.

Tosh played on a forward flank but he ran all over the ground, chasing the ball, which wasn't the done thing in those days, occasionally getting it and kicking wildly. If he was still alive today, he would claim he was the pioneer of the modern game. He came to where Simon and I were leaning against the boundary fence. "Keep your eyes on me, fellas. You ain't seen nothin' yet." He rushed back onto the field and elbowed his opponent in the chest behind the play and scrambled into packs from which other opponents crumbled to the ground. Later he leapt above a team mate to mark the ball twenty metres from the goals, which brought a roar from the crowd and blares from car horns. The kick went astray but Tosh didn't remember that after the game when he asked us if we saw 'the specky' he took.

"I saw you thumping them other players," I replied. "One of them they had to carry off."

He chuckled and Simon punched him affectionately in the rib cage. "You were great, Mr Tosh."

"Best on ground, don't you reckon?"

"Sure thing!"

Tosh ruffled Simon's hair. "Ah, you'd be a good son to have, Simo."

"Did you get reported?" Simon pleaded, hopeful, as if a suspension would be another feather in Tosh's cap.

"No, pal. It's all part of the game, isn't it? Umpires know that. A bit of biffo here and there don't do no harm. If you cry about it, you shouldn't be playing the game in the first place, right, Alan?" Now, he ruffled my hair, wistful rather than enthusiastic. "My boy's going to be a star one day, like his dad, aren't you, boy?"

When I responded with a shrug, he slapped the back of my head. "Aren't you?"

He wasn't pleased with my attitude. Football star was never one of my aspirations, but I was intimidated by him and shamed by Simon's sceptical snort, and so I agreed.

"I'll make a man out of you yet," he declared.

"You've got a job ahead of you there, Mr Tosh," said Simon with a wink.

Over the years Tosh tried hard to teach me the basics of football without success. Nor did he have much luck with other outdoor activities. When we played backyard cricket, my poor eye-hand coordination let me down. I refused to mount a horse the time he took me to a riding school in the high country for fear of it bolting down the mountain side, like the wild horses in the poem we had learnt at school. I finished last in the first-and-only go-cart race he insisted I enter. He raged when, a metre above the floor on the indoor abseiling wall, I froze, while Pam and Mum climbed above me. I could see disappointment lurking behind the anger in his eyes when he caught me reading after I had avoided helping him paint the shed in our back yard. The only activity I was happy to undertake at his suggestion was fishing.

He gave me a rod for my seventh or eighth birthday and took me down to one of the piers on Port Phillip Bay, where the sea was tranquil and the colours around me were subdued. I had no luck catching fish but that didn't bother me. What I enjoyed were the sounds of water lapping around the timber pylons and the gulls that waited for titbits. It was peaceful, too peaceful for Tosh, who was initially pleased he had found something we could do together but was frustrated with our meagre catches and soon got bored. After three or four outings around the bay, he stopped. "What a waste of time," he said. "I can walk to the shops and get fish and chips in five minutes."

My friendship with Simon ceased towards the end of primary school. It wasn't a falling out. He was killed by his father after his mother won a custody battle in the Family Court.

The murder was in the newspapers and on TV. Tosh was angry. What kind of father would kill his son? But he seemed angrier with Simon's mother. What kind of woman would drive her husband to murderous revenge? My mother, too, had something to say. "Oh, yeah, it's always the woman's fault." She spoke in a tone I didn't understand. I thought she was agreeing with him, as she always seemed to do. It was only later in life I recognised her fondness for irony that would largely go unnoticed by Tosh. "I'm sorry to hear you've lost your playmate," she said to me. At least this was sincere.

I got counselling at school, along with the other students, and then Simon was forgotten by everyone but me. I missed him, although our friendship had been rather strained towards the end. He had begun to steal things from me—colour pencils that he knew I liked, which I later found snapped in two, or my lunch box, which went into a rubbish bin—and he let down the tyres on my pushbike once and blamed it on someone else in an attempt to provoke a fight. But I saw no point in fighting and, besides, I knew the truth. Simon was trying to hurt me in his own way. He didn't want a best friend who wasn't as miserable as he was. Just before he was killed, I told him I didn't want to be his friend if he kept doing things to upset me. He swore at me, kicked out a few spokes of the front wheel of my bike, and sauntered away. It was the last time I saw him. I was upset he died before we had a chance to make up.

Tosh caught me crying. I was in his shed, looking for the wheel he said he would fix. It was on his bench, still with its spokes broken, which, of course, reminded me of Simon. When Tosh entered, I was sitting on an upturned metal bucket, elbows on knees, and my face buried in my hands.

"What are you blubbing about?"

"I miss him."

"Who?"

"Simon."

"You'll get over it."

"He was my best friend," I protested which descended into a howl.

"Oh, grow up, boy. You're embarrassing me. Are you going to bawl every time someone mentions him?"

"No," I sobbed.

"Be a man then. Shit happens. Help me fix these spokes. You said Simo kicked them in. What sort of friend was he, anyway?"

"He didn't mean to."

Tosh refused to let me go to the funeral. "It's not for kids," he said.

4

Be a man. How often did he tell me this throughout his life! *Be a man. Be a man.* What did he mean? Be like him? When I was younger I tried. I wanted to please him, but he mostly seemed disappointed or, at times, contemptuous. I watched him. I mimicked him. I strutted around. I tried to boss my sister. Unsuccessfully. I tried bossing Cassius, who ignored me. I tried playing football but wasn't much good at it. I was too timid. I couldn't see well enough without my glasses. I got hurt. I fumbled. My kicks went in the wrong direction. Once I had an asthma attack. Tosh said I probably wouldn't even make a good orange boy, whatever that meant.

For as long as I can remember, his opinion of me was poor. When I was eight or nine I thought I would build him something, as a surprise, to show him I could use my hands. Dexterity was important to him. And accuracy. About the only aspect of parent-teacher nights he enjoyed was looking at the artefacts that the best woodwork students displayed in the school foyer. "Why can't you do something like that?"

It took me weeks to complete the matchstick tray. First I found a good-sized piece of timber in Tosh's stack that required no cutting. The design needed the matches to be lit so that the red tips were gone. I spent hours striking the matches from the boxes I bought, one by one, blowing them out the moment they ignited to preserve them (without realising it was easier to light them all at once while they were still in the box and shutting the lid quickly to put them out), and then gluing them to the timber in a simple pattern. I tacked dowel around the edges, screwed on metal handles that I bought with pocket money, and gave it a lacquer finish after I found a tin of varnish in the paint cupboard. I was immensely proud of my achievement but anxious about his response. I waited until his birthday to give it to him.

He looked at my gift for a long time, frowning and then smiling. "You made me this?"

I nodded.

"Where? At school?"

"No, at home, in the shed."

His eyes widened with admiration. He must have been thinking: *Finally!* He turned it over to study the underside, and an expression approximating wonderment slid from his face like a cream pie. "Where'd you get this bit of timber from?" he almost whispered, hoping his guess might be wrong.

I hesitated. "From your stack. I didn't think you'd mind."

He stared at me in disbelief. "Oh, you bloody idiot!" He stared at it, turned the tray over to view the array of matches I had stuck to his timber, turned it back. "Me special piece of blackwood! I was saving it for a sideboard. Do you know how difficult it is to find matching shades of blackwood?"

My mother intervened. "Don't be hard on him, darl. He was just trying to please you. You can get another bit of wood, surely."

He looked at her with contempt, tossed the tray aside, and disappeared into his shed.

I never tried to please him again. But I observed him. As I grew older I observed him carefully so I could avoid turning out like him.

When I was about to start high school, Tosh was almost forty. He had friends who socialised with him on weekends, sometimes going to the pub or out to a restaurant, sometimes coming to our place to watch the footy or cricket on our big TV, sometimes playing backyard cricket, occasionally going away camping together, or attending the concerts of the Rolling Stones and other big-name groups still around from the Sixties and Seventies. But often, when it was just Mum and us kids at home with him, he was surly and short-tempered, barking orders at us or complaining or just sitting in his chair reading the sports pages of the Herald-Sun. Mum made excuses for him, saying he worked hard, he was tired, or his business was going through a rough patch, or he was worried about bills, or now Pam was a teenager, worried about what she might get up to, endless excuses for his increasing impatience with us. But when his mates turned up he always cheered up. He treated us affectionately. All a pretence, of course, for the benefit of his guests, who were under the impression we were one happy little tribe.

Mum played her part to perfection, making sandwiches and heating up pies for them, but otherwise keeping out of sight and ensuring Pam went to her room if she was at home, so they could behave like men do when they were together without the pressure of self-censorship that a female presence commanded. Tosh had a bar in the games room, along with a pool table, an old-fashioned pinball machine, and another large TV. There were a couple of old couches, with stains and a few rips, which Mum had tried to cover with throw-overs, but which never stayed in place once the men sat down. I was allowed to join them as long as I didn't bother them in any way and I fetched beer from the fridge whenever they wanted another.

I remember one day—while I was playing with my Game Boy and Tosh was watching cricket from a couch with a few

of his mates, including Uncle Darren, my mother's brother—
one of them asked me what I was like at cricket. He looked
around and called over his shoulder, "Aren't you interested
in the Test, Al?"

"Not really." I wanted to say test cricket was boring but I
knew it would irritate Tosh.

"What about the shorter form of the game?"

"Yeah, it's all right."

"Do you play, yourself? Are you in a team?"

Before I had a chance to answer, Tosh interjected. "Four-
eyes here, he's hopeless." He glanced at each man, a glint of
desperation in his eyes. "I've tried to teach him to bat. You
know how good I am. You think he might have it in the
genes. But, no, he'd get out middle-stump even if you bowled
a fucking beach ball at him."

"No, I wouldn't."

"Can't bat. Can't bowl. Can't catch." He threw up his hands
in a gesture of long-suffering disappointment.

When he realised his mates were embarrassed, he tried to
soften his contempt with a chuckle.

Uncle Darren came to my defence. He was fond of me
because he had no sons of his own but desperately wanted
one. "Leave off, Tosh, the boy's all right. He's just a bit
awkward, like most kids his age. Give him a chance."

"Give him a chance? I've tried to get him interested in
cricket. I've tried to get him interested in footy. I've tried to
get him interested in tennis, basketball, you name it. All he's
interested in is these computer games."

"Why don't you try playing them with him?"

"What, two can play, can they?"

"Sure they can, can't they, Al?"

I nodded.

"Well, I might just give it a go," Tosh said, surprised. "And I bet within a week I'll be able to beat him. He just doesn't know how to win anything."

Uncle Darren sighed. "It's not all about winning. It's about doing things together, with your boy."

Tosh snorted knowingly. "Oh, you poor sod, it's about winning, mate. Everything's about winning. You see, that's your problem, isn't it? That's why you've got to come over here and watch the cricket on *my* TV because all you've got is a little box, thirty years old or something. That's why you've still got a crippling mortgage, mate."

Uncle Darren shrugged, unwilling to get into an argument, but Tosh's pride was injured; he amplified the rhetoric. "That's why you've never been on a fucking cruise, mate, like the one I done with Alice last year, around the islands. Not enough drive, my boy. I know you've got a safe job, if you call pen pushing a job, but you don't take risks, do you? You don't invest in anything. You won't even spend a few bucks on a tatts ticket, for fuck's sake! You know something, Daz? You're in danger of becoming a fucking loser." He sniggered, swilled some more beer, and glanced at his mates to see if they were in agreement. When he realised they were staring elsewhere, he turned back to the TV. "If you're not already," he added, subdued.

"And what if I'm not hung up on winning? Words like *loser*, they aren't in my vocab, Ray."

"You mightn't see it that way, but every fucker's in the race, pal, whether you like it or not. Isn't that right, fellas?"

There were a few grunts but no clear affirmation. I could see Tosh was upset because he didn't order me to get him another beer but went to the fridge himself.

Surprisingly, after his argument with Uncle Darren, Tosh tried to change. He didn't try to learn any of the computer games, afraid he might not have been able to beat me, but suggested instead we go cycling together. He bought two mountain bikes. At first we rode along the path beside the creek near our place with him always leading the way and goading me to keep up. Later, when he realised we were both enjoying doing something together, he bought a rack to attach to the towbar on his car so that we could take the bikes into the countryside to follow rail trails or tracks in national parks, never quite abandoning his exhortations to race, but more out of habit than a genuine desire, for he was starting to appreciate the scenery, the tranquillity, the fresh air, and, I believe, the relief of having to prove himself to no-one, until finally it didn't seem to bother him if I rode ahead.

"I don't think you'd make much of a sprinter, Al, velodrome stuff, but have you ever thought of road racing?" he asked, one sunny day as we sat in a rest area at the end of a track.

"Nope."

"That's one possibility," he added, hopeful. "You're developing good racing legs."

"Really, Dad, I'm not interested."

He nodded, as if he understood, looking around at the mighty eucalypts giving us shade. "Just a thought, mate."

I hoped he was beginning to accept me, even if it was only on these occasions in the bush when there was no-one else around, without the presence of other men to prompt his acts of aggrandizement.

The cycling ended one day when Cassius, who used to run beside us along the track near our place, darted in front of Tosh and hit his front wheel. The bike flipped. I only wished

I'd had a video camera attached to my helmet as some riders do these days. The way he looped through the air and landed on his belly a few metres further up the track deserved a YouTube audience. Cassius was apologetic, slinking over to his prone master to lick him, and, another surprise, Tosh accepted the apology graciously, patting Cassius, whose body shuddered in appreciation. But with torn Lycra and skin off his palms and knees, he abandoned cycling for a more sedate form of recreation, namely lying on the couch at home watching sport on TV with Cassius curled up next to him. I still cycled after his mishap but alone. I can't remember us participating in any other activity together when I was growing up.

No, I'm wrong. There were two other occasions.

Mum went away one weekend to visit her sister interstate, taking Pam with her. Before she left, she prepared meals for Tosh and me to heat in the microwave. Tosh settled down for a day of watching sport. I settled down with a book.

I enjoyed Roald Dahl's stories and the crime novels of Agatha Christie whose murders I tried hard to solve before the end. Along with computer games and riding my bike, I enjoyed losing myself in these stories. Most boys my age never read. They hated it.

I started serious reading after Simon was killed. I had no other friends. I graduated to high school and was immediately singled out for special treatment by older boys, probably because I looked miserable and wore glasses, and I had grown tall but remained skinny, an odd shape for a year seven student. Many of the older boys already worked-out at gyms and by the look of them took steroids; others just ate junk food and were huge. They grabbed me near a toilet block on the first day, took me into a cubicle and thrust my head into a toilet bowl streaked with shit stains. They flushed it. Fortunately I kept my mouth shut, and my glasses didn't flush away. Because I cried afterwards and didn't try to retaliate, they saw me as an easy target whenever they wanted to exercise their superiority, which was often. My refuge was the school library. I soon realised I was different from most of the male students and, I liked to believe, cleverer, which saved me from clinical depression or worse.

Tosh occasionally queried why I read so much, worried it was softening my brain, but he never overtly disapproved. Instead he tried to lure me away from books.

"What do you think of girls?" he asked as we sat down in front of the TV to one of the meals my absent mother had prepared.

Such a delicate subject made me squirm. There was a girl in my class who had smiled at me recently, which made my chest constrict, but I was too shy to return the smile, much less talk to her. "They're all right," I said reluctantly.

"Is there a chick at school you like?"

"Not really."

He ignored my answer. "Has she got, you know, titties, boobs?"

I shrugged, unwilling to engage him.

"You like tits, don't you?"

"I guess so."

He picked up the book I was reading and waved it about. "Do you read about titties in this?"

"It's about twits not tits."

He wheezed his disappointment, left the room for a few minutes, returned, slipped a video into the recorder and settled on the couch.

Soon I was watching pornography from my armchair.

It was his way of dealing with his paternal educational responsibilities regarding the delicate subject of procreation.

I knew the rudiments already, having undergone sex education at school, but to view sex so starkly was a shock. Of course it excited me. I had never seen adult female genitals before, nor a grown man's erection, which looked too big to be real, ten times the size of my own. I could hardly believe my eyes when the woman struggled to put it in her mouth and almost choked. I was on the cusp of puberty. I felt my own erection convulse and a sticky dampness against my belly. I was mortified but Tosh hadn't noticed. He was watching the couple's antics and chuckling. "What do you think?" he muttered in a guttural voice. "You'll be doing that one day, my boy."

"Do you do it to Mum?"

He gaped at me, appalled, wondering how my mind worked. "Just watch the video, will you?"

I sank as far as I could into my armchair, trying to disappear. The male actor, if you could call him that, seemed completely contemptuous of the female actor, if you could call her that, and she seemed desperate to please him. He grabbed clumps of her hair and twisted her head around. He was brutal and unloving. Even when his cock squirted her in the face he seemed angry.

"What do you reckon?" Tosh asked, when the video ended.

"Why was he trying to hurt her?"

"Hurt her? Jesus, son, he was rooting her."

"I didn't think it would be like that."

"What did you think it would be like?"

"I don't know. I thought you were supposed to love each other."

He stared at me, incredulous. "Weren't you looking at her? She loved it!"

I retreated to the bathroom to stare at my irrepressible dick, with only the vaguest suspicion that my life had changed forever.

I must have been about fifteen, when we had another weekend alone. He came to my room where I was reading and told me to put on the suit my mother had recently bought me in anticipation of funerals. He called me a smart arse when I asked him who had died.

Tosh took me to a club in the city where men milled around outside. "Loosen the tie, will you?" he insisted as we approached. "Look smart but casual."

"Is he eighteen?" the doorman said, pointing at me. "He don't look it."

"Here's something to prove it," Tosh said, slipping him a twenty dollar note.

There was a lot of red inside—walls, doors, carpets, ceiling—and subdued lighting, except around these half-naked women on small platforms, swinging from poles, under spotlights.

Tosh led me close to one and said, "What do you think of her tits?"

"Dad!" I groaned.

He grabbed my arm, pulled me aside, and came close to my ear. "Don't call me Dad in here," he implored, barely audible, glancing around to ascertain if anyone else had heard me. There were men everywhere but they were rowdy and paying us no attention, their chins raised, their eyes focused on the cavorting women. "Use Ray or Tosh while we're here, will you?"

He pulled me back towards the woman on the platform.

"What's she doing?" I asked.

"Pole dancing."

"Why?"

"Oh, Jesus," he muttered, and handed me a five dollar bill. "Here, slip her this, and give her bum a touch while you're at it."

I looked at him horrified, reluctant to take the money.

"That's the idea, see? You're paying for a touch. Take it!"

I took it.

"Hey, babe!" he called.

The dancer, who looked young enough to still be at high school, maybe Year 12, noticed the bill I held and slid down the pole until her high-heels were on the platform. She kept hold of the pole and crouched with her bum towards me, smiling over her shoulder, waiting. I tried to hand her the money, but she tucked a finger under her G-string, indicating where I should lodge it. I quickly obeyed. She wiggled her rear end for a second, her way of saying thank you, and again scaled the pole.

"You didn't touch her up. What's wrong with you?"

"It didn't feel right, Dad."

"Not right? What are you talking about? That's what you were paying for. You didn't get your money's worth. Why didn't you undo her string? She would have liked that. God, boy, you've got a lot to learn. And it's Tosh, fucking Tosh or Ray, understand?"

There were other men crowding around, calling to the dancers, whistling and laughing. Most of them were in suits but they stank of sweat and booze, enough to make me gag. "Can we go?" I pleaded.

Tosh glowered at me. "Yeah. This's not why we're here, anyway. Come on." He guided me through the crowd towards another section of the night club, through a heavy door, into a theatrette, which was half-full of men. The stage was empty, except for a couch and a stool. Tosh led me to the second row. "You'll enjoy this," he said quietly, for the audience here was much more subdued than around the pole dancers. "All your mates at school will be dead jealous when you tell them where you've been this weekend, Al."

The lights in the theatrette dimmed and a couple of spotlights lit the stage. A boom of electronic music announced the arrival of two athletic men in suits, jerking around rhythmically right to the edge of the platform. They removed their jackets in unison, tossed them aside and kept dancing, until a woman emerged through a smoke haze, centre stage, dressed in a red sequined evening gown with a purple feather boa around her neck. She danced between them for a few bars of the music, and caressed the cheek of each man before one grabbed her boa and flung it into the haze. In a movement too deft for me to notice she unzipped their flies and extracted their dicks, already erect (with the aid of some drug, no doubt), and grasped them, a fake look of glee drawing her lurid red lips apart. Stunned, I stared as they just as deftly removed her gown and then her bra and G-string, and before long they were taking turns to fuck her, while she fellated the one waiting, shifting from couch and stool, trying to give the audience a view of their coupling.

I must had some kind of asthma attack. I collapsed between the seats, gasping and wheezing. Tosh tugged at my suit, demanding I get up. Desperately I searched my suit pockets for my puffer, flailing my limbs, disrupting the entertainment's climax. I inhaled the salbutamol until my breathing settled. Someone arrived with water, which I sipped while he berated Tosh. "Get him out of here. He's only a kid, for fuck's sake!"

Outside, after a humiliating exit, Tosh strode back to the car, hunched and muttering, while I followed behind, still sucking on my puffer. I could tell he wanted nothing more to do with me. In the car he gripped the steering wheel but wouldn't look at me. "Here I am, wanting you to grow up knowing what life's all about, and what do you do? You have a fit on me!" His voice was high-pitched, indignant. "Christ, I don't know what sort of man you're going to grow into." Then he voiced his worst fear. "You're not a fairy, are you?"

"Course not," I rasped, thinking he was referring to those folkloric creatures I'd seen in picture books. I took two more profound draws on my puffer.

He pulled into the traffic, causing some anger from other drivers, and headed home. "Don't go and blab to your mother where we've been, all right?"

5

I thought he would give up on me after the strip club episode, but, perhaps with my assurance I wasn't a fairy, he acted like we'd formed a manly cabal. He'd wink at me and smile when the female members of our family had their backs turned or left the room. It unnerved me but I tried to reciprocate, lest he take umbrage at my sullenness. He started a private conversation about how it was okay to sow some wild oats while I was young, whatever that meant—I had no interest in farming—but eventually I'd have to settle down and raise a family, and that would require finding the right woman, a decent woman, like my mother or sister, not them of course, but like them. And no decent woman wanted a man who couldn't provide her with all the worldly comforts. So, had I given much thought to what I'd like to do with my life?

"I'm talking to you about this now because the earlier you start thinking about it, the better." He puckered his mouth and squinted to indicate he was serious. "And you know what I'd like, don't you?"

It wasn't hard to figure. "For me to do something like you do?"

He pouted and nodded, pleased we were finally in accord. "The reason I'm working so hard and setting up this business is for you, Al. You're not going to let me down, are you?"

I felt the dread rising in my stomach. "I'm too young," I moaned.

"Before you know it, you'll be grown up. A man." He grabbed my chin and inspected my face. "Look at the bum fluff on your lip. I better get you a shaver or you'll start to look like a hillbilly. If you're going to be a businessman one day, the sooner you start looking like one, the better."

He handed me a wad of money. "Go buy yourself some good quality gear, not that cheap stuff your mum buys you. And get some runners that'll make all your mates jealous. I want you to start looking your best. Looking like a success is half the story. You start by impressing your mates."

"I don't have any mates."

He gaped, incredulous. "Sure you do, son." He shook his head, as if trying to remove an insect from his ear. A moment passed. His eyes were shut. His lips were moving as though in prayer. When his eyelids sprang open, he grabbed my arms and started to shake me, scaring me, before he came to his senses and hung his head in what seemed to me a gesture of profound disappointment. "Just get top-shelf runners and you'll have plenty of mates," he muttered as an afterthought.

Later on, perhaps after he realised runners alone would do little to elevate my popularity, he suggested I forget about finding friends. "Now you're in high school, Al, concentrate on your studies. There'll be plenty of time for mates once you're in business. If you're a success, they'll stick to you like dog shit. But you need a good head for numbers."

"I'm not much good at maths."

He grimaced. "Keep on top of it, pal. I'm a natural, but you, you're more like your mother. You'll have to study real, real hard. Do they do economics at your school? Do that. And I reckon you might even get to university, something Alice or I never did. You can do an MBA or something. That'll be good for the business."

Maths, economics, an MBA were the last things I was interested in. I enjoyed English and Art and not much else. I hung out in the library during recesses and lunch breaks, and after school I went to the local public library or my hideout near the creek, and not just to avoid other kids, but because I loved books. I read sci-fi and fantasy, anything to cloak reality. At home I read as well or played computer games.

Perhaps it was his musing about my future that led Tosh to the idea that the one franchise he controlled was not enough. He eventually purchased another in an outer suburb, a rash decision on account of its distance from the first, not to mention financially. His solution, which took another year for him to realise, was to buy a new place for us to live, halfway between the two chicken joints, in a swisher neighbourhood, not far from the Chadstone Shopping Centre, a retail monster that gorged on shoppers. The new home was an old house, a large dark-red brick dwelling, built at the start of the last century. It had a porch at the front with solid, partially rendered arches, and a front door with stained-glass panels. A passage ran through the centre of the house, past a living room and three bedrooms to a dining room, a huge kitchen, and a recent extension, which Tosh designated a games room. The rear of the house overlooked a long sloping backyard with an English garden. Except for the extension, it was not the sort of house we were accustomed to. But he had social aspirations. I think he hoped that the expansion of his business interests and taking up residence in an affluent neighbourhood would somehow automatically generate wealth. Likewise, ownership of a luxury SUV on top of two other vehicles—a van for the franchise and a run-around for Mum—and the enrolment of his children in elite private schools would hasten his climb up the social ladder. Regrettably, all these merely placed greater strain on his finances, stretched his credit to the limit, obliged him to employ a manager for one of his outlets and a supervisor at the other, increased his blood pressure and doubled his intake of nicotine and alcohol. But initially he was optimistic and this translated into a period of calm in the household, which I welcomed. He took me aside one day, put an arm around my shoulder, and told me he was doing all this for me. "You're going to have your own chicken outlet," he said proudly, giving my neck a squeeze.

"It doesn't matter what I want, does it?" I muttered, one of my first acts of defiance.

He appeared not to hear me. "Just a few more years."

"What about Pam? She could run it better than me."

"I've got something else in mind for her."

Although I was upset by the abandonment of my childhood home and suburb, the familiar bicycle track and creek and my favourite secluded spot for reading and latterly for wanking, I was relieved at least to find Tosh was soon too busy to bother me much more. He rose before dawn, shaved and showered, plucked protruding nostril hairs, combed his thick fringe over the eyebrows, slapped aftershave onto his cheeks, sprayed antiperspirant towards his armpits, and put on clean pressed shirt and trousers and, finally, his jacket with its rooster insignia and company peak cap, which he straightened and adjusted before the bathroom mirror until the angle was just right. I observed this on the odd occasion when both the doors to my bedroom and the bathroom were ajar. He never ate breakfast. At that time of day the house was quiet. I heard him put on his shoes at the front door and depart. I heard the motor and then the van reversing from the driveway soon after. It would be dark again before he returned.

My mother wasn't entirely happy with the new location either. She was left to place all her favourite trinkets and pictures, gathered over the years from Trash-and-Treasure markets and garage sales in the northern suburbs, into a house totally unsuited to her tastes. The effect was startling. Even I, at my young age, could see it. But I left Pam to point it out. "Mum, it looks gross," she said of the large posters of Mick Jagger about to devour a microphone and a bare-chested Jim Morrison, both behind perspex and hung from an old-fashioned picture rail against the panelled walls of the living room. The orange moon lightshade and Friesian calf skin rug, which had suited our previous home perfectly, seemed crass in a room with a ceiling rose and a parquetry floor. "How can I bring any of my new schoolfriends here?" Pam moaned. "They'd just laugh."

Within a week of starting at her new school, Pam had been accepted into an exclusive group of popular girls. Unlike Mum and me, she was delighted with our changed circumstances. She quickly adopted the attitudes, manners and even the posh accent of her new friends. Fitting in with them required a new wardrobe and a better range of cosmetics, which she soon acquired on shopping forays with our mother and our mother's credit card, a solace for Mum and a shock for Tosh once he received the monthly bank statement, although he quickly understood the value of his daughter's "investments", as canny Pam explained, even accepting her advice with regard to the posters, the rug and the moon lightshade, which were shifted into the games room to be replaced with quality reproductions of classical artworks—Velázquez's *Equestrian Portrait of Count-Duke of Olivares*, Turner's *Decline of the Carthaginian Empire*, and for the passage walls some reproductions of anatomical sketches by Leonardo da Vinci—all in elegant timber frames and recommended by her art teacher, Ms Roselyn Farnell-Jones, on whom Pam had developed a raging crush during her first art class at the new school.

Roselyn—I took the liberty of calling her by her first name when Pam introduced me—Roselyn came to the first barbeque Tosh oversaw at our new place. He had invited some of his business associates and a few mates from the old days when he was a butcher, tradies mostly whom he still accompanied to the footy and the cricket, although as his business connections grew, he was more inclined to seek invitations into corporate boxes at various stadiums around the country, hoping to fraternise with club presidents and well-known business figures as well as a few celebrities without a tradie in sight. Mum invited a couple of friends from her old aerobics class, plus her brother, Uncle Darren, who seemed to appear at all our social gatherings. I invited nobody.

Roselyn was the most conspicuous guest, since her hair was spiked and purple, and she must have acquired her dress-sense from the Old Testament, except she wore platform shoes and a cluster of bangles on each forearm, rings on every finger. I wondered how such a reputable school as the one in which she taught would employ someone as outlandish as her. But it paid lip-service to the liberal arts and what better way to show its tolerance than with an art teacher like Roselyn. Pam and a few invited classmates followed her around like faithful puppies, while she chatted with them but gravitated towards the tradies.

I watched from a safe distance, sitting on the timber rail around the decking that had been installed at the same time as the games-room extension. Tosh was on the other side by the barbeque, hovering over sausages, chicken wings and onion rings, with the supervisors of his franchise outlets deputising in aprons, employing spatulas and prongs beside him. My eyes did not linger on them or my mother, who was sitting and chatting with her friends under the pergola, but trailed after Roselyn and her retinue of school girls, trying to imagine what they would look like without their clothes. Ever since my visit to the strip club I couldn't cast my eyes at a female without mentally undressing her, even my sister (with the exception of my mother, of course, whose nakedness would have horrified me). Although I felt guilty and sordid, I couldn't stop myself. Half my days awake and most of my nights were spent with an erection. Since the girls were a year or two older than me, I was of no interest to them. Their eyes, like Roselyn's, were on the tradies, or so it seemed. I imagined them in lascivious acts before I willed myself to look away, back to Tosh instructing his deputies to flip the chicken wings.

Since the strip club excursion I realised Tosh had his faults. His paternal authority began to falter. I no longer thought he was a stern demigod whose attitudes, actions and judgments could never be questioned or criticised. Throughout my childhood we had been at odds about almost everything, but I had been under the delusion that it was my problem, not his. As a teenager this changed. Completely. His persistent attempts to make me his protégé, his insistence that I would inherit his business, and his belated camaraderie, as if we were in manly collusion, were anathema to me. I became hyper-critical, more than the average teenager, I suggest. I watched Tosh. I looked for faults. I looked for behaviour I could excoriate.

"Not joining in?" It was Uncle Darren, who had seen me sitting alone and sauntered over.

"Look at the wanker."

He seemed to know who I was talking about. "You shouldn't call him that." Yet despite his reproof, he couldn't help chuckling. "He's your father, Al."

"Look at him lording it over them other two. Why doesn't he flip a few chicken wings himself?"

"Someone's got to do the hard stuff," he joked.

"Yeah, well, it's not him, is it? It's never him."

"I think you're being a bit unfair. He's worked his butt off to get to where he is."

"And where's that? Lord of the B-B-Q?"

His smile lingered while he cogitated. "You're a smart kid, Al, very perceptive," he replied, perhaps with some sarcasm of his own. "But you're still just a kid. Do you know how hard he's worked to make your life easy? I mean, look at this place. And the school you go to. You got any idea how much he's spending on you? You ought to be grateful."

"It's all for my benefit, is it?"

Uncle Darren was a chubby person with a thick, droopy moustache, looking like a lot of cricketers of that era: avuncular one minute and fierce the next. I waited for fierce.

"No," he enunciated in a ponderous manner. "There's a fair degree of self-interest at work—ambition, pride, prestige—but he does care about you and your sister, and your mum."

"You're the last person I thought would stick up for him."

"I'm not sticking up for him," he sighed. "I'm just making a few observations, that's all."

"Yeah, well, you don't have to live with him."

"True, but whatever you think of him, he's still your father. It's a special thing, buddy. He's the reason you're here."

"What, thirty seconds of excitement is all it took him." I heard my voice rising shrilly. "And I'm expected to be grateful the rest of my life?"

I felt my uncle's aversion. He pulled away from me. "You can be as bitter as you like, Al, but it's poison. You let it linger for too long in your system and you'll be a lesser person for it. You'll grow up stunted. There's plenty of men like that around. They don't need another to swell their ranks."

Despite his anger he smiled at me, put his hand behind my neck and squeezed affectionately before he walked across to help at the barbeque. I glowered with too much burgeoning audacity to allow his words to shame me.

For the rest of the afternoon I considered myself superior to all and sundry, observing Tosh, his underlings, his working-class mates he preferred to call tradies, my mother and her girlfriends, my uncle, the schoolgirls and their quirky teacher, as if they were my laboratory specimens. No bigtime entrepreneurs, I noted, with whom Tosh hoped one day to mingle.

No-one could shut up for a moment. It was constant babble, the cacophony of wannabes, each one trying to impress the next. But none worked at it harder than Tosh. He wanted appreciation, sought it, and, except from me, he got it.

After everyone else had been served at the barbeque, I helped myself to sausages and sat alone. For a while the men played kick-to-kick in the backyard, away from the women, where Tosh was able to demonstrate his marking skills with triumphant roars and cries. "Fellas, did you see that specky?" "Tosh takes another screamer!" "Eat my dust, you losers!" He had a litany of self-praising exclamations, which the other blokes found rather tiresome. But Tosh only felt their admiration. Afterwards he insisted they all take a beer and follow him around his new abode so they could see what an astute investor he was, as well as a proud family man. Some of the woman tagged along.

Before they went inside, I heard him say, "Alice and the kids love it here. What a gem, eh? You won't get a better example of a Federation Home—yeah, I know me architecture, and yous all thought I was just a pretty face, he, he! But that's not all. Wait and see, in ten years' time this property will have tripled in value, maybe even quadrupled. It's location, location, fellas. It's within walking distance of Chadstone, and that place is just going to grow and grow until it's ginormous, the biggest bloody shopping centre in the entire southern hemisphere, if not the world. Can't you see what that's going to do to property values around here? If you've got any brains, you'll follow my example. Buy up now. Mark my words, you'll make a fortune just sitting on your arse."

His mates didn't disagree with him about property values, which might just as easily decline due to the amount of traffic and noise such a shopping complex generated. They followed him inside to inspect the rooms, and when they re-emerged, he stood before them on the decking and pointed to where he intended to put a swimming pool. "The pergola will have to go," he declared. "But who cares? It's an ugly thing anyway."

The women still sitting under it got up and moved away.

Unable to endure any more of his gloating, I went to my room to play computer games.

6

I had to catch a train to school each day. The school was closer to the centre of the city in a suburb where Tosh had hoped to buy a house but was thwarted by a market value designed to keep lower-level aspirants in their proper place. Nevertheless, he could brag about his son attending one of the most elite private schools in the country, still with an all-male student body, in a sprawling edifice worthy of aristocratic England, perched on a lofty knoll, surrounded by Olympic-standard sporting facilities and curated English gardens. But appearances can be deceptive, as they say. The genteel setting was a veneer over something baser. And since my family's economic status by the school's standards was lowly and I arrived without a sporting or intellectual reputation halfway through the first semester, I was fair game for its prefects, who cornered me in the male toilets, much like my first day in the state high school. But instead of a dunking—nothing so barbaric!—they removed my trousers and underwear and ridiculed the size of my dick, which had shrivelled in fear, as several of them held me down on the tiled floor. With a warning not to disgrace the school, they left, taking my trousers and undies with them.

"Just another day in enemy territory."

I heard those words as I sat shivering in one of the cubicles. It wasn't cold as much as trepidation that shook my body. My trousers dropped at my feet, thrown over the door by a sympathetic student who must have witnessed my humiliation, or participated and felt guilty, or found them discarded somewhere outside the toilets, and in his kindness came to my rescue. I put them on without underpants, which were still missing, and tentatively emerged to meet and thank Patrick, an odd-shaped teenager in a shabby school uniform, standing with his legs splayed and his hands behind his back, scrutinizing me.

"You'll find the undies on the student noticeboard. It's a custom."

I nodded and grimaced, struggling to hold back my tears.

"An initiation thing." He added. "A prefect ritual. Most of us have been through it." He wobbled the glasses resting on his diminutive nose. "I'm an iconoclast. I oppose everything these blackguards do. My life is currently devoted to disrupting their training."

I had no idea what *iconoclast* or *blackguards* meant. "Training?" I asked, mystified, thinking my father had enrolled me in some sort of military academy.

"Cadetship for the ruling class."

Noticing my puzzlement, Patrick frowned while he thought of a way to explain. "For the elite that run this country. We're taught to believe we live in a democracy. Do you believe it? Don't believe it. Don't be brainwashed by the propaganda you see every day on TV, in the papers, on the radio, and in this indoctrination centre." He waved his arms around, gesturing decisively. I thought he meant the toilet block but apparently he was referring to the rest of the school as well. "The power elite controls them all. Everything, everywhere. It's a charade. It's a farce. And the sooner you realise it the better, comrade."

"Comrade?"

"*Comrade*! Meaning *friend with the fellow oppressed*," he replied proudly. "It's from the lexicon of the downtrodden."

So grateful for his support, I was happy to endure his weird way of talking.

He took me out of the toilets, led me across the grounds to a remote corner where some bushes grew and introduced me to a couple of his schoolmates, Jonathan and Damien. "Join the club," said Jonathan, with a smile that lifted one half of his face when he heard what had happened to me. Damien offered me a cigarette.

Jonathan had black hair and an olive complexion. I could see evidence he already shaved. There were bristles on his chin and he had grown slim sideburns in the shape of gaffs, which at the time, in the late nineties, were fashionable. Patrick, whose belly strained the buttons on his grubby white shirt and made his blazer look several sizes too small, had blond curly locks, flaccid cheeks and large moist lips, which looked like they had spent the last few hours savouring meats and wines at a banquet. But Damien was the winsome one. He had sun-bleached hair, a permanent melancholy smile and tragic blue eyes. The three of them were in Year 11, two years ahead of me.

"Did you get a digital probe?" Damien asked.

I looked at him blankly.

"He was spared that, at least," said Patrick.

I noticed some chairs, purloined from classrooms apparently, and a wooden park bench, purloined from somewhere else. I lowered myself onto the bench and the others sat on the chairs. Jonathan handed around a cigarette lighter.

"We're the resistance," Patrick declared.

"Jonathan was digitally examined and so was Patrick, on their first day," Damien added. "I was one of the lucky ones. I managed to avoid the full induction. Like you, I only lost my underpants. Perhaps they were too pushed for time when it was my turn. But I witnessed what happened to others."

They asked me some personal questions about my age and background, reciprocating with information about themselves, which I took to be an attempt to engender trust. Jonathan was the son of a business consultant and his mother, as it happened, owned a boutique at Chadstone Shopping Centre, a store I had wandered past a few times, close to another franchise that Tosh had his eyes on. They lived in Camberwell. Damien's parents were academics who lived in Parkville. Neither boy sounded downtrodden. As for Patrick, he refrained from imparting personal details, which he considered irrelevant.

"I focus on the big picture, comrade," he announced when I looked at him and waited for his contribution. "I haven't got time for trivia. Individualism is a game the ruling class plays."

Damien once again put his hand upon my shoulder. "There'll probably be more bullying in the weeks ahead," he predicted. "Anyone, like you, starting in the middle of a term is an easy target, especially for those who were bullied at the start of the year. It's their chance to redeem some of their injured pride."

"Wrong target," Patrick snapped. "We'll mount a counter-attack."

"Oh, yeah, that's going to happen," Jonathan responded deadpan.

"If you hang out with us in the breaks you should be all right," said Damien. "After school we'll walk with you to the station."

Which is how our friendship started, despite our age differences.

If I hadn't met these three, I would have gone home on the first day—assuming I was able to recover my pants—and begged Tosh to find me a different school. I was especially drawn to Damien whose phlegmatic temperament reassured me that the whole world wasn't against me. He assumed the role of my protector and must have had a word to some of the prefects, who approached me on subsequent days to apologise in a roundabout way, trying to explain their involvement as a rite of passage.

Damien tried to deny any role in their expressions of contrition, but I suspected he had used his influence. His parents were professors at Melbourne University in the History and Literature Departments, and they had a long association with the school. Perhaps the prefects feared Damien could somehow undermine their higher education admission prospects. I would never know. I wasn't privy to the machinations of influential people.

The professors travelled each year for months at a time to exotic locations, like Tierra Del Fuego, Outer Mongolia, or Central Australia. In their absence Damien had the family home more or less to himself. He was an only child who was looked after by an unreliable aunt whenever his parents were on one of their treks. The aunt was a gambler who disappeared for days on end, encouraged by Damien to do as she pleased. In her absence he invited friends to stay.

After Damien and I left the school as soon as the day's lessons were over, instead of heading for the train station we caught a tram to Parkville. Damien lived in a double-storeyed Victorian terrace on a quiet street lined with bare plane trees.

The interior of the house was gloomy. A long passage down one side was a repository of books and bicycles. Tall bookcases, with more books than a family could read in a lifetime were only separated by framed anti-war posters, and another of a bearded dude called Che in a beret, whom I later learned was a legendary revolutionary from Cuba. The two front rooms off the passage were lined with bookcases as well. Each room had a large desk, a swivel chair and a computer, and again the walls had framed pictures: more protest posters and prints of paintings by Kandinsky and Miró. Original artwork, a Fred Williams' landscape and a smaller urban-scape by Jeffrey Smart, were displayed in the sitting room, and then there were limited-edition Salvador Dalí and David Hockney prints above the cane settee and the upright piano in the sunroom at the rear of the house, next to more bookcases. None of these artists meant anything to me, with the exception of Dalí, whose wilting clocks had caught my attention once in an artbook at school, but I would get to know them eventually through Damien and his small circle of friends. In the meantime, I was overwhelmed by the exotic ambience of the house. It was shockingly different to any other I had been in.

Damien sensed my unease. "Not so many books at your place, eh?"

"Here I am thinking I've stumbled into a bloody library."

"Nope, just a hoarder's house, when it comes to literature at least."

"Who reads them?" I asked in awe.

"My mum, my dad. I've read some of them. Do you like reading?"

"Yeah."

"Well, if you want, have a look around. You can borrow one or two if you like, as long as you bring them back."

I was unsettled by his trust; it wasn't something I often experienced.

The books in the sunroom were all paperbacks but not the sort I was used to reading, more highbrow, I thought. I pulled a couple of them off the shelf and looked at the covers. One of them had a dull silver cover with no clue to its contents and was called *The Catcher in the Rye*. "Have you read this?" I asked.

He nodded. "It's a coming-of-age thing. Losing your innocence or keeping it, I can't remember. You might like it."

I sat on the settee and began to read.

"Would you like a cup of tea?"

Surprised he was not offering a soft drink or even a beer, I paused before I said, "Milk, two sugars, thanks."

As he left to put on the kettle, I started reading and was already several pages into the novel when he returned with a tray supporting two cups and a metal cake tin. Expecting shortbreads, I waited while he placed a cup on the side table near me and moved to another cane chair beside the French doors that opened into a courtyard. Instead of a biscuit, he took cigarette papers from a packet in the tin, licked a couple and stuck them together. With the other contents of the tin he manufactured a joint, taking his time, as if it were a work of art. I had never seen one made before, so I watched carefully, thinking it might be a useful skill to have. When he finished, adding a crude, rolled cardboard filter to one end and twisting the other to a point, he lit up, sucking noisily, dragging a lot of smoke into his lungs and holding it there, longer than I expected. The room filled with an unfamiliar odour. His eyes were closed. When he exhaled a funnel of smoke entered the room, and he rose from the chair, reluctantly it seemed, and reached across to me with his eyes still shut. I took the joint, studied it for a moment and then sucked on it as resolutely as he had. His eyes sprang open, I'm sure, when he heard my reaction. I gagged and spluttered and gasped. I swore and coughed. "Fuck, what is this stuff?" I managed to utter, my voice an octave higher than usual.

"Go easy. It's quality dope, man."

The quality was destroying me. I was totally at its mercy. When my coughing fit subsided I fell into a swoon, unable to raise my head from the settee. Damien came across and took the joint. "You ever smoked before?"

"Cigarettes," I whimpered.

"Dope?"

I hesitated, reluctant to reveal my inexperience, but eventually shook my head, which in itself was unwise because my brain started sluicing inside my skull, inducing a wave of nausea. "Fuck," I murmured. It rolled through my body, a tsunami of humid numbness, far worse than my first cigarette. I felt totally in its power. But I lay still, determined to master it, unaware in this inaugural moment that it would eventually, one day, master me. I accepted the joint again after Damien had taken another toke.

Later in the day, while I was still unable to move, Damien spoke. "It might be a good idea if you stayed here tonight rather than go home in your state." I could hear music from Nirvana's *Nevermind*, my favourite album, which Damien must have put on at some point. "Why don't you ring and let your folks know what you're doing?"

I had only slept away from home once before, at Simon's place, and only then with permission from my mother. The thought of telling her or Tosh I was staying over at a friend's place gave me pause. I was about to make a decision about my own life, a momentous event, my first real act of maturity. As it turned out I didn't tell either. Damien handed me a cordless phone. I rang and Pam answered.

"Dad will be ropable," she said after I asked her to pass on the message. "You sound funny. Is that your asthma?"

"No," I squeaked.

She laughed and hung up.

I'd been slightly worried about my asthma, but the dope didn't induce it.

I mentioned this to Damien as I handed back the receiver. "Marijuana's a bronchodilator," he said and added, when he noticed my incomprehension, that it was good for asthma sufferers.

I looked around. My eyes could easily discern shapes in the courtyard despite the absence of daylight: a potted cumquat tree, a cat licking itself nonchalantly on top of a cast-iron table, a relief sculpture attached to the brick garden shed. A wave of euphoria washed over me, buoying me on the soft cushions of my chair, but it receded the moment the front doorbell rang.

Damien strolled off to answer it. I sat up and tried to clear my head, overcome with fear that Tosh had traced me to Parkville and was on the doorstep.

Jonathan and Patrick entered.

"Looks like you've recovered from your ordeal quickly enough," said Jonathan.

I grinned with relief and giggled.

"He's been smashed all afternoon," Damien answered with a chuckle behind them. "Hasn't said much. I think it's the first time he's smoked."

"Speaking of which," Jonathan enthused, "time for another, wouldn't you say?"

And so began another session, about which I remember very little, except that Patrick didn't participate. Instead he drank wine and smoked cigarettes, his head buried in a tome he collected from the study of Damien's father. The other two took no notice of him, left him in peace to read, while we smoked dope and listened to *Nevermind* over and over. At some point the aunt came home, took one look at us giggling and arguing about the meaning of the lyrics, asked Patrick, whom she decided was the least intoxicated, how long we had been at it, to which he answered with an estimate of several hours and added that his friends couldn't cope well with reality, before she disappeared into her room to suffer her losses alone.

7

This is how my life spun out of the orbit of my family, how my dependency on marijuana began, how a mental illness crept up on me, none of which I anticipated at the time. Perhaps I should have taken my cues from Patrick, but he was detached, indifferent to us as individuals, only ever interested in us as victims of oppression, symbols of a wider malaise, a wider struggle than personal frailties and insecurities. Over the next few months I became close to Damien and Jonathan, spending most of my time with them, angering Tosh who expected me to contribute more to the family activities he considered important, like mowing the lawn, or pulling down the pergola, or joining him in front of the TV to watch football.

We went to clubs around the inner suburbs where bands from the alternative music scene played. We dressed in black jeans and leather jackets and combed our hair over our foreheads, in the old Beatles style, a bit like Tosh's, in fact. I tried my hardest to look like The Verve's lead singer, Patrick Ashcroft, and to match his insolent mood in the video of *Bitter Sweet Symphony*, often removing my glasses so I wasn't mistaken for a geek, although I was worried about tripping. I stayed at Damien's as often as I could, smoking dope, staying up late and watching *Rage*, or listening to 3JJJ. I met the professors, who were personable enough but aloof, accepting my presence without questioning me about my parents and what they might think of my absence from home, treating their own son like a border rather than their child, passing through the same space, but living in a different psychosphere. If I stayed overnight I slept in the guest room, which was upstairs. It had French doors onto a balcony overlooking the street. Often Damien and I would sit out there, especially when the warmer months returned and the verdant canopy of the plane trees offered the street some shade. We would smoke cigarettes and drink his parents wine. We would talk about music or the countries we would like to visit or the movies we had seen, or art, for we occasionally went to the NGV to view the contemporary part of its collection. Jonathan would often join us on the balcony. He and Damien had passion for art history and for hours could discuss the evolution of different artistic styles or the lives of artists I had never heard of. I listened in awe, hoping one day to be as knowledgeable as they were, reminding myself they were two years ahead of me. But if Patrick was with us, the conversation invariably turned to world affairs. He would lean against the cast-iron latticework and say something like, "Look at you lot, dissolute progeny of the privileged class, idling in a house that's worth millions, drinking vintage wine, slurping caviar. Do you know that more than half the world's population lives on less than a dollar a day? And how much does that caviar cost, huh? Thirty or forty bucks? No, you wouldn't know about such a trivial matter. Caviar? Mummy pays for it. The day's coming for you lot when the masses rise up—". On and on he would go. The personal segueing into the global. Yet he never refused a wine when it was offered. Nor did it seem to bother him that he came from a family that had more wealth than the rest of ours put together. His father had made his millions, probably billions, on currency speculation. The family had a mansion in Toorak. And each year his parents took him and his siblings on holidays to the Mediterranean or the Caribbean. You would think he would be happy the way the world was, given he wanted for nothing, but Damien told me that it wasn't a matter of happiness with Patrick, who never seemed miserable or depressed or anxious. For him, the way of the world was far beyond his control, a mere individual. The march of history was determined by the formidable economic forces at play. The vast hordes of humanity, the exploited masses, would determine the future, not Patrick Graves, not Damien Mattison-Henshaw, not Jonathan Smythe, nor Alan McIntosh. To be on the right side of history, all we could do was resist the forces of oppression and agitate for change.

Patrick had read *Das Kapital* at his family's holiday retreat near Portsea over the Christmas holidays when he was fifteen, had found errors in a few calculations in Volume III, which he attributed to Engels, who had compiled the volume from Marx's notes after the scholar's death, but, overall, he was impressed by the theory, despite weaknesses in its analysis of the State. He forwarded the errors to the few universities around the world that still taught Marxism, and offered to forward any more he discovered after his second reading. He was not an iconoclast, in this instance, but a stickler for accuracy. As for an analysis of the State, whose complexity Marx had badly underestimated, he recommended Lenin's *The State and Revolution*, which I graciously declined and instead accepted from him, on the basis of its length alone, *The Communist Manifesto*, "liberated" from the Mattison-Henshaw family library. Despite its brevity, it remains unread somewhere in my book collection, unreturned to the professors, with whom I no longer have contact. My intention was always to read it before I took it back. But years have passed and that course of action now seems absurd.

The truth is that neither Damien, Jonathan nor I had much interest in politics or ideology. We didn't view our school as a capitalist conservatory nurturing future captains of industry, against which we fomented insurrections as a precursor to wider social upheaval and an eventual revolution, as Patrick asserted. It was well past the era when student politics flourished. Rather, our rebelliousness at school was motivated by our feelings of injustice and the minor tyrannies that should never have been tolerated in a venerable place of learning. Why were Damien and Jonathan friends with Patrick? Well, he had no other friends and they felt sorry for him, and, I have to admit, he brought our little coterie a degree of notoriety that we were happy to accept, as it lent each of us, myself included, undeserving status amongst our fellow students. We were labelled *the mavericks*, which suited us fine.

I was about to write *kudos* instead of *status*, but that would be an exaggeration, a misrepresentation. We were not liked. Other students were offended by our flouting of school rules and traditions. The way we refused to wear our ties straight. Our refusal to have our blazers dry-cleaned or pressed. Our refusal to polish our shoes. The time we wore mascara, which caused an outcry. Our truancy. Our refusal to stand for the national anthem, which caused an even louder outcry. We were ignoring a sacred duty to represent our school in the best possible light in the public domain. And word got around that we attended picket lines in support of striking workers, which we did twice, in school uniform, at Patrick's behest. In other words, we were trashing its reputation, 'trashing its *brand*," Patrick corrected while he farted long and loud. But all our recalcitrance was insignificant in the course of world history. "We're facing the greatest crisis ever," he declared with unflappable optimism. "There are no checks and balances on the imperialists anymore. The Soviet Union is gone. Okay, not a great example of socialism, nevertheless a restraint on what the Yanks could do. But now? You wait, comrades, the Gulf War was only testing the waters. Big toe stuff. They'll be back there before long and the whole Middle East will explode. It's all about oil which keeps the capitalist machine lubricated. It's now up to the American working class to rise up against its masters and cripple the war economy."

"Yeah, that's going to happen," Damien muttered, ironic as usual.

"You know that song, *War?*" Jonathan added, and so steered the conversation towards a topic the rest of us knew something about. Music. He sang the chorus. "Know it? There's a lot of versions. The Temptations. Frankie Goes to Hollywood. Bruce Springsteen. Some black guy did it first, I think. And there's that other song, *Eve of Destruction?*"

Damien nodded solemnly. "Midnight Oil still does *US Forces* at its concerts. What a classic! It's still a crowd pleaser."

A discussion of Midnight Oil's contribution to the Australian music scene ensued. Patrick lit a cigarette and leant against the balustrade, looking at the plane trees, his thoughts elsewhere, while Damien and I shared the bong that Jonathan prepared.

I was often stoned when I arrived home, usually late at night, trying to avoid Tosh, who rarely stayed up after ten, exhausted from the stress of running his two chicken joints on opposite sides of the city.

One night he was waiting.

"You stupid bloody idiot! Your mother was right. She reckoned you were on the drugs. Look at you! You're off your face!"

He looked like a gargoyle: mouth agape, venting animosity; eyes bulging, as rigid as stone.

I started to giggle and didn't see his fist coming. It smashed into my face and burst my bottom lip like an overcooked sausage. Bubbles of blood formed when I gasped. I tried cursing him but it was blood and saliva, not words, that issued forth and sprayed him. I heard his roar and nothing else.

He must have hit me again.

In the morning I was on my bed, still in school uniform, even in my shoes, my mouth aching, the back of my head split and sore, unable to remember how I managed to reach the bed or whether someone had helped me. As I stirred, the pain intensified. My tongue discovered loose front teeth, which upset me more than the split lip and cracked skull. I lay there a while, my vision blurred, my head throbbing, slowly assessing the damage. I moved my jaw sideways and suffered the consequences. Shards of pain struck my eyeballs and filled my sight with phosphorescent light. I lay still, too scared to move again. Minutes passed. I felt my limbs—arms first, then legs—squeezing gently. They were okay. My belly was sore. I figured Tosh's second or third punch was to the stomach. I pressed it. More pain. I relented, lay still for another five minutes, before my bladder demanded attention.

Getting to the bathroom was like a trek across the tundra. I hobbled from my room and slumped onto the toilet bowl and pissed and shat and blubbered, my legs shaking, snot dripping from my nose. I stayed on the seat long after I had finished, unable to muster the energy or will to wipe my bum, until the bathroom door swung open and my sister entered. I heard an apology, and then a yelp of shock when she noticed my condition before I could focus on her. I was beyond protesting. Besides, it would have been hypocritical; I had spied on her often enough from a branch in the tree outside the bathroom window, when she showered in the evening.

"Shit, what happened to you?" she cried.

"See what a caring father we've got," I slobbered. "He's helping me give up the drugs."

"You're on drugs? Jesus!"

"I smoke a bit of weed now and then, that's all. Don't you?"

"Well, yeah, once or twice, but—." She paused and watched as I began to wipe my bum. "Can't that wait?"

"Don't let him catch you stoned then," I muttered.

"He did, once, but he just ticked me off."

"That's typical, that is." I tried to rise but couldn't. "Give me a hand, will you?"

She took my hand and steadied me. I doubt she had ever seen me without pants of some sort. She graciously refrained from any derisive remarks and helped me towards the vanity basin. "Have you seen yourself in the mirror?" she asked. "That's some black eye."

I was shocked. "I can't go to school looking like this."

As she stood beside me, scrutinizing my reflection, she squeezed my buttock, in sympathy I hoped. "Have a shower, brov. It'll do you the world of good. I'll help you get undressed."

"No, no," I moaned. "I can do it."

"It'll be a lot easier if I helped. Besides, it's only fair, isn't it? I know you're a little perv."

I denied it, of course, but she merely hissed in disgust and insisted on divesting me of my modesty. "Well, well, we're not a little boy any longer, are we?" she said when I was naked.

I dropped a hand to cover my genitals.

"Don't be so prudish," she said in the offhand tone of a nurse. "Do you think this's the first willy I've seen?"

"Who else's?"

"None of your business, little brother." She took my arm, led me to the shower and turned on the taps.

I wailed because the water was cold. But it soon turned warm and I was grateful.

"I'll get your robe," she called above the sound of the water. "And, don't worry, Dad's already gone to work. So stay home today."

"Thanks, sis," I said later when I was tucked up in bed with a cup of tea.

She offered to get me some toast until I revealed the state of my teeth. "Most of the time he's a good bloke, but you just bring the worst out in him," she said, straightening her school uniform. "Then he can be a bastard."

"Yeah, I know, it's all my fault."

She ignored my sarcasm. "I've got to go, but Mum will be back soon."

Half an hour later my mother made an appearance. "What are you doing still in bed?" she scolded.

When I raised my head to look at her, she said, "Oh, my God!" She hastened to my side and place her hand on my forehead, as if to take my temperature. "Who did this to you?"

I could smell her sweat. She had been on her morning jog, or whatever she did first thing in the morning, and was still in her pink tracksuit and runners. Her hand was hot and sticky, useless as a thermometer.

"Who do you reckon?" I muttered through my loose teeth.

"Those guys you hang out with at school? They look capable of murder to me."

"Tosher," I corrected.

"Tosh? Your father? When?"

"Last night when I came home late."

"Because you were late? He never mentioned it when he came to bed."

"Because I was stoned."

She took her hand away. In an instant her expression changed from maternal concern to parental disapproval. "What have we told you about taking drugs? This is serious, Al."

"So is assault."

"Yes, but you've got to learn."

"What, knocking my teeth out and splitting my head open is your idea of an education, is it?"

"Oh, Alan, I don't like your snitchy attitude. You've become very arrogant since you've started at this new school. Those boys you hang out with, they're a bad influence. I wish you'd dump them. There's plenty of nice boys at that school, I've heard." She stood and adjusted her pony tail. "Stay in bed today, darlin'. We'll talk to your father about it tonight. It's not like him to hit you, is it? You've got to realise he's under a lot of pressure, keeping his businesses going."

"And whose fault's that?"

"There's that snitchy attitude again. You never used to be like this. He's only doing it so you can go to a good school."

"Bullshit, he's doing it for himself. Nobody else."

8

She was right, I never used to be snitchy. And I was right, he was only doing it for himself. If he wanted Pam and me in prestigious schools, it wasn't for educational reasons but to impress others. If he wanted to run two chook joints when one was difficult enough, ditto. The same with the Federation House. The same with everything. By the age of fifteen I had figured it out: he needed everyone he knew to admire him—no, no, not to admire—to envy him. He needed it as much as he needed oxygen.

My mother arranged a meeting with him later that evening, where he explained his use of violence. His demeanour was sombre. Right from the start he wanted me to understand that he didn't get any enjoyment from punishing me. It probably upset him, more than it upset me. But it was for my own good. I would realise that when I was older and had developed a few brains. Better to nip a curiosity about drugs in the bud before I got addicted. The severity of his attack on me was proportionate to the seriousness of the problem. Okay, he was prepared to concede punching was a bit excessive, but I would end up on the streets, homeless, begging, or worse, in a Bali prison awaiting execution, like some other stupid Aussies, if I didn't wake up to myself. One day I would thank him for his warning.

"What about Pam?" I mumbled. "She didn't get a beating when you caught her."

"She's a girl," he declared, exasperated at having to state the obvious.

He went on to explain once more that what he wanted from me was to follow him into business, not necessarily taking on his franchises, although that would be ideal, that would make him immensely proud. He was actually trying to acquire a donuts franchise store, for me to run eventually at Chadstone Shopping Centre in conjunction with Pam, if that's what she wanted. He thought donuts would suit me more than chickens. That's all he wanted out of life: a happy family and a son who was eager to follow in his father's footsteps. He warned me to stay away from Damien and Jonathan or he would withdraw me from the school, which would be a great shame because the alternative didn't bear thinking about: back to a State school. Tosh had cultivated an aversion to anything—institution or service—the government provided.

"You can decide your whole future right here, right now, buddy," he concluded, jutting his pimply chin forward, his reptilian eyes retreating into lifeless cavities under his Merseyside fringe.

I cast my gaze at the table and avoided a response.

"Don't sulk! That's what girls do. If I ever catch you with drugs again, it won't be a black eye and a few loose teeth—"

"What'll be?" I interjected. "Murder?"

"Get him out of here, Alice," he said, "before I do some serious damage."

My mother was an ostensibly obedient wife. She accompanied me to my bedroom. "Please, darling, think about what he's saying. He really wants to set you up in a business. He means good. Look, can I tell you something, your father and I are no angels, right? When we were younger, we smoked. A bit."

"What, dope?"

"Yeah. Only a bit. All young people do it, don't they? It's fun. I agree. But the thing is to know when to give it up. Tosh, his father would've beat him up if he'd ever caught him. But he had the good sense to stop before that happened. I know you don't listen to your mum much, but let me give you this advice. If you're going to smoke it, don't come home stoned, all right? It only upsets your father. And don't smoke too much. You'll get hooked. There's nothing worse than dope addicts. They sit around all day doing nothing, totally useless."

I looked at her anew, seeing her as a person and not just a mother, with a youthful past, unknown to me. She had smoked marijuana. And so had my hypocrite father. I wondered what other transgressions she had committed. There was still a hint of youthfulness in her physique. And the beauty creams she used assiduously had so far kept the wrinkles at bay. I could see she must have been attractive. Boys other than Tosh must have been interested in her. I wondered if she'd had sex with any of them. Surely she had. I wondered why she had settled on Tosh. Okay, he probably would have been handsome and athletic. He might have looked like one of the Stones, probably the one that drowned. But there must have been some other reason. You don't commit the rest of your life to a marriage on physical attraction alone. That surely was a train wreck waiting to happen. Thinking of them with lives that extended into the past beyond my existence was disconcerting. She might have gone off with some other bloke and I might never have been conceived. I started to feel incidental rather than the key ingredient of the universe.

Everyone at school, including my teachers, wanted to know how I received two black eyes and a split skull. I told them all, even my three school friends, I had been set upon by delinquents who wanted to steal my expensive footwear. Their failure to accomplish the theft earned me some kudos.

The teachers' reaction was predictable. They asked me if I'd contacted the police. I thought of telling them I could exact my own retribution but realised it could have unintended consequences. So I lied again to mollify them.

After school I went with Damien and Jonathan to share a joint on the south bank of the Yarra River near the Botanical Gardens, looking across at all the sporting arenas. It was a balmy day which allowed me to be generous in my opinion of Melbourne. No doubt the dope helped. I could see beauty in all the buildings and even the khaki colour of the Yarra. And Jonathan, not normally disposed to lyricism, was reciting poetry from a new book about the streets of Melbourne by an anarchist poet. I lay back on the grassy embankment to listen to him while I watched the drift of clouds above the office towers with only the occasional twinge from my injuries to remind me of Tosh.

"My old man beat me up," I confessed to them when the poetry reading finished, inspired by its raw honesty, "for coming home stoned."

Damien propped on his elbows and regarded me with an ambivalent smile. "So that story about the mugging was bullshit?"

I winced, knowing how he hated people lying. "I didn't want the whole school thinking my father was a prick."

"Why not? He must be to do that to his son," he said in a matter-of-fact tone. "If you spoke up about it some others might too. There's plenty of fathers like yours. Jonathan's father is not exactly a paragon of virtue."

"Neither is yours," said Jonathan, a tad defensive.

"No, true. While mine would never physically attack me, he's a master of psychological cruelty."

"I think he's great," I said. "He leaves you alone. You can do whatever you want."

"It's called neglect. He's totally engrossed in the academic world, in his career, his reputation, his status at the university. He's got no time for me. He thinks that by putting me in a prestigious school he's accomplished his role as father and needs to do nothing else except take me on a tour of Europe now and then, which would be fine if he didn't turn it into a research sabbatical. Library after museum after university after library after—."

That didn't seem so bad to me. So I kept my own counsel and allowed him to feel aggrieved. A flat-roofed river launch, full of Chinese tourists, cruised past. We sat quietly and watched. When some of them noticed us, they waved. Damien reciprocated and Jonathan held the joint aloft, as a symbol of Western freedom.

"If we ever need a collective name we could call ourselves the Damaged Sons Club," Jonathan suggested, after the cruiser was gone and he had taken a long toke. "We could probably recruit plenty of others, the entire student body, for example."

"The entire adolescent male population of Melbourne," said Damien and took a noisy drag on the joint.

"Of Australia." I added and took a drag.

"Why so parochial?" Damien spluttered, as smoke and words mixed.

The club was formed by our impromptu committee on the banks of the Yarra with the sole criteria for membership a genuine complaint about one's father. Yet, despite our wildly optimistic predictions, it never grew larger than four, thanks to our apathy. Patrick was included, although he offered no criticism of his billionaire father. Individual angst was of no concern to him. He urged us to read *The Origin of the Family, Private Property and the State* by Friedrich Engels, which would add some broader perspective to our minor, neurotic grievances, giving us the opportunity to submit our personal circumstances to a class analysis. And, no, Engels, as the co-founder of communism *and* a wealthy industrialist, didn't strike Patrick as a hypocrite when Damien pointed it out. "He was a bourgeois, no argument there," replied Patrick, "just as we are, but sophisticated progressive thought was never going to emerge from the oppressed, uneducated masses. It took enlightened scholars like Marx and Engels and Lenin to analyse the big picture."

I felt sorry for Patrick. His dismissal of everything personal as unimportant struck me as his way of coping with a deep-seated loneliness. Nobody liked him, probably not even his father. We tolerated him but he was never close. There was no strong affinity. Perhaps, if he had smoked dope, things might have been different.

But then he was the first to find a girlfriend, which really surprised us. For Jonathan, it was more than surprise; he was indignant. "How come he pulls a chick before you or I?" he muttered to Damien. "A lard-arse like him?" he added in an uncharacteristic display of bile.

"Because we're shy and don't try hard enough," Damien mused.

That made us all laugh a soft yearning sound.

But the truth was Patrick hadn't found a girlfriend, she had found him, at a rally for the unemployed, where he had given a rousing speech about surplus labour and the role it played in maintaining the impoverishment of the working class. She was a junior research officer with one of the unions, earnest and bespectacled and four years his senior, which didn't bother Patrick. In fact he wasn't even aware of her age until Jonathan pointed it out to him, months later. Jonathan had asked her, suggesting she might even be breaking the law if they were having sex, at which she smiled and said, "Who'll ever find out?" "Can't you find someone your own age?" "Do I detect jealousy? One of your mates is getting some and you're not?" She chuckled. "Anyway, he's mature, well beyond his years, unlike some, comrade." "Don't call me *comrade*. I'm not your comrade." "Yeah, you're right. You're a spoilt rich boy." "Patrick's richer than I am!" "Oh, grow up, will you."

It infuriated Jonathan. He pinched his long, narrow nose and scowled behind his hand. Some inner demon inflamed his eyes. He wanted us to break with Patrick, who had failed to criticise his father, sufficient grounds, he asserted, for expulsion from the Damaged Sons Club, but Damien wasn't interested. He considered Patrick a noble soul, unfazed by the opinions of others, which was a rare quality, a person who had principles and stuck to them no matter how unpopular they were.

Jonathan took Damien's response as criticism and kept to himself for a while. But a week or so later he dropped by the Victorian terrace with a schoolgirl in tow. Damien and I had taken the afternoon off school and were sharing a joint when he arrived.

"This's Jodie," he said, his face beaming with triumph and relief. "Can we use the spare room for a while?"

Damien looked at them for a moment, appraising the situation, concealing his surprise. "Have you got a condom?" he asked Jonathan.

Jodie answered. "I have."

It would be almost another year before Damien found a girlfriend, the enigmatic Tiffany Sutherland, leaving me as the last virgin in the Damaged Sons Club. It didn't strike the others as a crisis. After all, I was two years younger. But, thanks to Tosh, I knew what I was missing out on and felt deprived.

Tiffany was into writing, poetry mostly but also prose, mainly in her diary. I never saw her without it. She often brought it out, in the middle of conversations and wrote a few lines, which fascinated me. She also encouraged me to do the same, giving me a notebook and an expensive pen. "Don't worry what others say. Don't worry about what you think. Write what your heart dictates." I blushed at her generosity and took her advice, becoming an intermittent diarist.

With girlfriends occupying much of their time and a sudden devotion to study in the final year at high school, my friends wanted to see less of me. It took me a while to realise I was often intruding. Damien offered me sachets of dope to smoke in solitude while he and Jonathan were dating their girlfriends or swotting.

Indulging alone was a dangerous pastime. I found a place to do it away from prying eyes, in a shed near the back fence of an ailing widow in our neighbourhood, who was no longer capable of traversing the depths of her property, and which I accessed from a lane and through a gap in loose palings. The shed was a place full of cobwebs and rusting garden tools, but there was a perished plastic garden chair to sit on and a broken card table that I managed to erect and wipe relatively clean, on which I could prepare joints and place my notebook with the intention of spilling my heart onto its pages. The heads Damien supplied were potent. One joint would leave me stranded on the chair for most of the afternoon, with erratic, maudlin introspection amusing me one moment and distressing me the next, some of it reaching the page, but not a great deal, the pen seeming too heavy, until, famished, I would slink home and raid the pantry for biscuits and cakes and tins of sardines. I would take the repast to my room to avoid anyone else in the house, where I tried to get straight before dinner.

Fortunately, Tosh was mostly absent for meals, thanks to the demands of his franchises, but eventually he learnt of my irregular school attendance, my poor grades, and my antisocial attitude in class activities. Halfway through my Year 10, he decided not to waste any more of his hard-earned money on private schools fees for me, and had me transferred to the local high school, where at least I wasn't subjected to any humiliating initiation rites and there was some deference shown once I spread the rumour that I had been expelled from one of the most exclusive schools in the state. I thought Damien, at least, would have been upset to see me leave his school, but there was no farewell party offered and none of my classmates commiserated when I announced my departure.

In my new environment I remained aloof, partly because some of the elitist attitudes fostered at my previous school had rubbed off on me, partly because I was grieving the separation from my friends, who had moved on anyway, who had found girlfriends and knuckled down to study, to ensure they got into uni. The Damaged Sons Club seldom met, and when it did the others made scant mention of it, and certainly didn't come to it with the same gravitas as I did. To them it had become a stale joke and they were quite annoyed when I kept referring to it. Even my supply of marijuana began to dry up, Damien making excuses, telling me the plants his parents had allowed him to grow in their small backyard had been stolen. The little he had left in storage he was keeping for his own consumption with Tiffany. Only Patrick seemed to treat me with the same regard, which had never been particularly personal. And, while I was impressed by his indifference to my fate, he had never really been a fully-fledged member of the Damaged Sons Club. His friendship was less important to me than Damien's and Jonathan's. He was peripheral.

Months would pass at the new school before I found another supplier. In the absence of my preferred drug, I began to steal Tosh's whiskey. He had a few cases of Jim Beam in the cellar beneath our kitchen, contraband he'd received at a heftily discounted price. I'd open the trapdoor, concealed beneath a heavy rubberised mat, and sneak down when nobody was home. I figured he wouldn't miss a bottle now and then, which I stored in the widow's shed and went each day to drink. I soon became dependent upon it.

At the new school I was a loner. I liked to think it was of my own choice, but a kid approached one day and said nobody wanted to come near me because I stank like a *wino*. He shocked me but I scowled and told him to fuck off. I walked around the schoolground like Patrick Ashcroft, with only my glasses compromising the image. In class I sat at the back without a set of eyes behind me. Other students thought I did nothing but idle my time, sullen and silent, until the bell rang so I could leave and get another drink, but I was actually studying hard, following the teacher's every word each lesson, taking notes, reading texts. And no matter what subject—maths, English, history, economics —when the teacher asked me a question, expecting no answer, hoping to show me up since the staff all shared the students' opinion of me, I would give the correct answer. I was never fulsome, never showed off my mastery of the topic at hand, although it was obvious I knew far more than I was prepared to share with the class, until the teachers refrained from asking more, unless they suspected I had fallen asleep. Behind my secretive diligence was a yearning to get high enough VCE levels to go to university and reunite with Damien and Jonathan.

At the end of classes, one day, as I was passing through the school gate to go home, or, rather, to head for the widow's shed, a student approached and asked me if I smoked dope. Suspecting idle curiosity or more mockery I didn't stop, but she strode beside me and clasped my arm. "Hey, dude, I'll get you an ounce, if you want." My stride faltered. I looked askance at her. My impression was she wasn't joking. She had the appearance of substance abuser of some sort. Heavy makeup in defiant colours: green and orange and black. Greasy, wispy hair. She had a crooked nose and thin lips, but I liked her eyes, which were cat-green and slightly cross-eyed. Her smile was lopsided too. "No bullshit," she said.

I nodded but kept walking.

She sidled up to me and put her face close to mine. "Won't be a jiff, Mr Cool." The smile lifted one side of her face, a freakish contortion. She hastened away, across the street and further along to a parked car where she spoke through the back passenger window for a moment, stuffed something into her parka and returned at a casual pace.

It took her a few minutes to catch me. "Hang on, dude," she called, annoyed. "Do you want this or not?"

I said nothing but slowed my pace until she was next to me.

"Well?" she insisted, trying to get an answer from me.

I stopped but still said nothing, waiting for her to announce how much it was going to cost me.

"People might be right about you. They reckon you're an arrogant prick. But I like to make up my own mind. So?"

I just stared at her, observing her skinny figure. She looked anorexic but that just made me suspect she was using harder drugs than marijuana.

"Fifty bucks," she said.

I only had ten dollars. "I try before I buy," I said with my mouth barely open, which made her smirk.

"Okay, where?"

I motioned with my head for her to accompany me and headed for the widow's shed.

"Whose place is this?" she asked, sounding anxious as she squeezed through the fence.

"You're not scared, are you?" I mocked.

She shrugged and followed me into the shed, cast her gaze around, saw my empty bottles of whiskey, and said, "No wonder you smell like a dero."

I shifted some tools on one of the shelves and took down a tin that contained my smoking paraphernalia, including a small glass bong, which I placed on the card table. I sat on the only chair and put my hand out for the sachet of dope she had in her jacket.

"You don't say much, do you?"

I didn't answer.

"What's your problem, dude? I'm trying to be friendly. You haven't even asked me my name."

"You haven't asked me mine."

"I know yours. No-one's-pal-Al, that's what everyone calls you."

"No-one's-pal-Al?" A cynical chuckle curdled in my throat, but secretly it hurt. "What's yours then?"

"Sky."

"What, Sky, like out there?" I pointed at the window, which was a frame for spider webs, with the scene beyond barely visible.

"Yeah. So?" Her tone was defensive, accusatory, as if she expected ridicule.

I put out my hand for the sachet. "Let's try this skunk." I was attempting to sound indifferent—jaded, even—as if all the small talk that preceded a deal bored me.

I didn't get the sachet, not straight away at least. Instead she lunged at me, grabbed my jaw, and forced her tongue into my mouth. I fell from the chair onto the filthy floorboards, and she tumbled on top of me, squealing.

"Shit, shut up!" I hissed. "Granny might hear you."

She responded by smothering my mouth with hers and somehow getting a hand between us and squeezing my balls. My body jerked in shock. The only way I could hide my embarrassment was to grab her scrawny breasts and squeeze until she gasped. We were still in school uniform. She wore a tunic. I put my hand under it and groped for her panties. In the frenzy that followed, she assisted in removing them and helped undo my pants. She hoisted my dumbstruck dick out of its nest and only spoke to ask if I had a condom. "Never mind," she said and climbed aboard as I lay amongst the debris and dust. I ejaculated before I could say *wait a minute*.

"God, you didn't last too long, did you? Like about two seconds! Have you ever done it before?"

I pushed her aside and struggled with my trousers. "I've got better things to do."

"Ooow!" she howled and sniggered, as if she had guessed the truth.

That's how I lost my virginity, gained a girlfriend and a new supplier in one fell swoop.

The dope was expensive. I had to purloin any money I could find lying around the house, in drawers, in pockets, between couch cushions, in Mum's purse, which she kept in a drawer near the front door, and Tosh's wallet when he was whiskey-snoring in bed. A few times I hocked ornaments and some old Christmas presents I no longer wanted, the most expensive being a Rolex that Tosh had bought me when I started at the elite school. Why keep a memento like that?

Sex with Sky was good. She liked fucking and found a better place than the widow's shed to do it. She had a key to her elder brother's flat, which had a mattress on the floor and some dirty sheets where a few more stains wouldn't be noticed. Her brother had a job and was never around while we were using it.

She was all bones. Her hips and knees were as hard as granite, and when she was standing her thighs failed to meet at the crotch, leaving a gap through which I once watched the sun go down while she stood before a window, awakening the poet in me. Her breasts weren't much bigger than mine, but what was surprising was the amount of pubic hair she had. I thought, with her head of wispy hair she wouldn't have much down below, but when I got my first good look I was amazed. Soft and profuse, the dark strands were long enough for me to twirl and grasp and tug, which made her groan and become aggressive. She would force me down and climb on top, barely giving me time to put on one of the condoms I managed to buy at a supermarket, before she bore down and worked her pelvis like a steam piston, hurting and scaring me with her urgency. She also enjoyed sex from behind or standing, options we took when we were not in the flat, but she never wanted me lying on top of her, perhaps because of her physique. We lasted about six months before she said she was sick of me hanging around her, which was a surprise because I thought she was always hanging around me. There was no animosity between us but no love either. Fortunately, by the time we went our separate ways, I knew her dealer.

9

I was back smoking bongs in the widow's shed, lamenting Sky's absence, but disappointed that she had been ripping me off. I discovered she had charged me ten percent more for the dope than her dealer had sold it to her. Once again I resorted to masturbation for sexual relief and was working hard at reaching a climax when the cops arrived.

"Put your hands up, you filthy little bastard," the first constable in the door said. I obeyed. "No, no, do us a favour." She pointed with her truncheon at my groin. "Tuck that little thing away first."

I was then handcuffed and led to a divvy van in front of the house. The fearful widow watched me through a window. She had seen me sneak through her back fence and rung the cops. I gave her a resentful stare as I passed. Her fear was never going to match mine. I thought they would lock me away for ten years.

Being a legal minor, I was told my parents would be notified. Tosh came to the police station and was present at my interview. We sat side by side behind a table on which a glass of water stood, alongside a recording device awaiting to catch my confession. Two police sat opposite. Tosh didn't say a word to me, didn't ask if I was okay, didn't ask me what I had done. My mouth was parched but I was too intimidated to reach for the glass. My hands would shake water all over the table. The next ten years in jail was the only thing I could think about.

The cops started asking me questions about what I was doing and why I was in the old widow's shed. I mumbled something about nowhere else to go where I could be myself. No, home wasn't a place I could feel that way. Did I mean *feel myself*? (The cops were enjoying my humiliation.) Not *feel* myself, I meant *be* myself. And why was that? I gave an apprehensive glance askance at Tosh and answered with a shrug. They didn't ask me to explain, probably because they heard similar excuses from most juveniles they interrogated. They asked me where I got the dope and I lied, more scared of my dealer than a long prison sentence. I told them I found it, along with the bong, abandoned near the local creek and that I had never used drugs before in my life. It was just adolescent curiosity. I would never do it again because it made my head funny. And what about the empty bourbon bottles? They placed one, already in a plastic bag, on the table as evidence. I shrugged and suggested it belonged to the widow. But Tosh recognised it. I felt his body stiffen. This was when he began to talk, agreeing with me about my misdemeanour being a silly adolescent adventure that would certainly not happen again, he would see to that. I came from a good home, he was a respectable businessman, who operated several franchises, and, by the way, if they were ever in the neighbourhood of one of his outlets, they could just drop in for a complimentary meal, for the police did a great service for the business community and deserved a whole lot more credit than they ever received. And, if he was in government, not that he wanted to be because he didn't have much time for politicians, but if he was, his number one priority would be to look into police remuneration levels and do what he could to change negative community attitudes towards the force. Tosh deftly removed some business cards from the inner pocket of his suit and gave one to each cop. His Gauci suit was an astute touch, I thought. It would carry some weight with these lowly upholders of the law. "I give you my word," he concluded earnestly, looking into the eyes of each cop separately, lingering, hoping they understood his sincerity. "I can deal with this. I'll nip it in the bud. No son of mine is going to end up a dope fiend. Hand him over to me and you'll not see or hear of him again."

I should have been grateful, but when the cops turned off the recorder and left the room to confer, Tosh turned to me and said through his teeth, "Have you any idea what this does to my reputation, you little crook? You're going to regret dragging me through this, mark my words."

After fifteen minutes the cops returned and released me with a warning: next time the matter would go to court. Did I have any idea how a criminal record would impact on my future? "We don't want to see you back here, boy. We won't be so lenient next time," the senior cop said. The other one just narrowed her eyes and trapped me in her memory. "You're lucky you've got a father who cares for you."

They ushered us out, ignoring Tosh's attempt to shake their hands. His anxiety seemed the only positive outcome of the whole sorry episode.

In the car I pleaded with him. "Honest, Dad, what I told them was the truth. I haven't used marijuana for ages." My voice was plaintive but unconvincing. "You've got to believe me."

"What about my bourbon? Sneaking into my cellar, you little fucking thief! Don't think I hadn't noticed my supply going down, but here I was thinking it was Alice helping herself. I should've known I couldn't trust you as far as I could kick you!"

"I'm seventeen, Dad!" I bellowed. "I should be allowed to drink." It was a feeble defence but I wanted him to understand I was growing up and didn't want to be treated like a child.

The rest of the trip home was in silence.

The assault began the moment I was through the front door. Tosh was behind me. He started slapping me around the ears. My glasses flew off. I swung around to defend myself, using my hands and forearms to ward off his blows until he punched me in the mouth. Through tears and blurred vision I struck back, flailing my fists, hitting mainly his arms but once catching his cheek, which startled him. I was taller but he was much stronger. He swung me around, put me in a headlock, and shunted me into the games room. When he knew I had an obstacle in front of me, an old-fashioned footrest, he thrust me forward, over the top of it. I hit the floor hard, lost consciousness for a moment, and came to as he hoisted me from the floor by the collar.

"This's for your own good," he said, before shoving me over the footrest again.

The next thing I was aware of was the taste of blood. My face was pressed against the floor boards. I opened my eyes and saw my arm was at a strange angle and the flesh above the elbow was bulging. I studied it in a detached way, feeling no pain, but thinking it must be broken. Then I lost consciousness.

My mother shook me. She was frantic. "What's happened to you?"

I managed to blame Tosh, who had disappeared. She helped me to my feet. Now the pain arrived with such force I almost collapsed again. She led me to her car and took me to hospital, where they gave me morphine, an X-ray to confirm the break, an operation to insert a titanium pin, and finally a bed in a private ward thanks to Tosh's prudent family medical insurance cover. I texted Damien and Sky explaining where I was, since neither of them answered my calls. It was a long shot with Sky, since we had split up, but I was hopeful Damien, at least, would respond. Both of them were sentimental and I didn't think either had reason to dislike me. Only Mum and Pam came to visit.

The hospital doctor wanted me to stay a couple of days to run some tests. I had a long gash in the back of my head, which Mum said was the result of my fall. "He's always tripping over things, poor boy," she added. "He's short-sighted but won't wear his glasses. Vain. And look how tall and gangly he is." Through the sheet she tapped my feet, which reached the end of the bed.

I spent hours in the ward alone feeling sorry for myself. I had no real friends to speak of. Nobody really cared for me. I hated my father, who had made my life an ordeal, despised my mother for her cowardice, suffered my sister's indifference. Pulling the sheet over my head, I cried for a while, which gave me some comfort. And when my tears dried up I watched TV.

When the scans of my brain showed no damage, I was discharged from hospital and took a taxi home. My mother was busy with a community fundraising event, Tosh was at one of his chicken joints, and Pam was at work as a shop assistant somewhere in the Chadstone Shopping Centre.

I was depressed, which felt physical rather than mental, as if there was some kind of vice around the nape of my neck that I couldn't reach to loosen. I stayed in my room. I didn't want to go back to school. My arm in a sling made me look vulnerable. I still had some dope, hidden in the toe of one of my runners. The joint I made was massive, as big as a turd. I hoped that by smoking it in a hurry the depression would release its grip and be replaced with pleasure, even if it were only temporary. Instead, within minutes, I found myself bawling and regretting my whole life. Nobody loved me. Nobody cared for me. I was nothing to anybody. Just background noise. If I disappeared inexplicably nobody would notice until they wanted me to do something, like put out the garbage, or clean up the dog shit in the back yard. And only old Cassius appreciated that. I began to think I was worthless. People took no notice of me because I did nothing to be noticed. I did nothing outstanding or unique. That was why Tosh despised me. He wanted me to be a success at something, preferably sport or business. But I didn't have a competitive bone in my body, which he interpreted as cowardice or laziness, or both. Maybe Tosh was right. I was as useless as *tits on a bull*, as he so eloquently expressed it. Maybe I should just do him a favour and end my life. He wouldn't miss me, nobody would, a few perfunctory motherly and sisterly tears that last maybe a week, and then the lives of the McIntoshes would return to normal. Tosh would be relieved, even grateful. I buried my head under the blankets and entertained various ways to kill myself.

There were overdoses with sleeping tablets or even heroin, which I could get my hands on easy enough. There were cuts to the wrists with a razor blade, a hose in the exhaust pipe of a car, a leap in front of a train or tram, the sea or a river or even a bathtub in which to drown, a plastic bag over the head, a bullet into the brain. None of them really appealed. Most of them would take some organising, would take time, and I would be sure to lose my nerve. Nevertheless, in a piteous state and wanting my whole family to feel guilty about how they treated me, I decided to attempt something.

I was alone in the house. Tosh and Mum both used sedatives, which they kept in a bathroom cupboard. I decided to swallow the lot. To be doubly sure of a successful outcome I incorporated whiskey and wrist-slitting into the plan. But the only razors in the house, which belonged to Mum or Pam to use on their armpits and legs, were impractical. Tosh used an electric razor. And he had bought me one for the day I reached manhood. I was yet to start shaving seriously. What bum fluff I had looked like a feeble attempt at a goatee. I detoured through the kitchen to collect a glass of water and the sharpest knife I could find. I took a half-full bottle of bourbon from the games room. The folklore around slitting wrists was that it was best done in a warm bath, so I turned on the taps and found the bottles of sedatives in the medicine cabinet.

Ingesting a hundred tablets was harder than I expected. I gagged a couple of times but managed to swallow most of them. I took gulps of the whiskey. Then, removing the sling but not my pyjamas—not wishing to be found naked—I took the knife and lowered myself into the rising water. With the titanium pin in my arm, I had no plaster cast to hinder me. I was already feeling drowsy when I started cutting my wrists. The pain was localised, nothing like a fist in the face, whose force enveloped the skull and undulated down the spine, as if, like lightning, it needed to earth. Blood streamed into the water and spread. I watched the water turn pink with a detached curiosity. The last thing I remember of the experience was thinking nobody would miss me. I felt tremendously sorry for myself and glad to be going.

10

I woke in a hospital bed, nauseous, sore, disoriented, confused, amnesic, with my brain feeling like it was about to explode. I tried to look around but the glare of lights made it difficult.

I was lying on my side towards a wall. A voice, full of cheer, thundered over me. "Wakey, wakey, you lot! Brekkie time!" There was a zinging noise, blinds drawn, and more unwanted light entered the room. I lifted my head and squinted. The voice belonged to a huge islander dressed in a nurse's uniform.

This time I was not alone but in a ward with three other patients, who were inanimate and unidentifiable, hidden under sheets. The nurse saw I was awake. "Mr McIntosh," she called, the first time I had ever been called mister, "how are you feeling this morning?" But she wasn't expecting an answer. She began to shake the others. "Come on, you lot, I've got work to do. Wakey, wakey!"

I turned over gingerly.

The others stirred. One of them, a gaunt man in the bed next to mine, sat up and looked around the room until his gaze reached me. His eyes narrowed as they observed my face, trying to make a determination, which he reached when they settled on the arm that I had pulled out from under the sheet. When I followed his gaze and saw a bandage around my wrist, I remembered what I had done and groaned.

He called to a patient across the ward in a voice sounding like it emanated from a deserted underpass. "Here's another one of your lot."

The patient whimpered.

"Wrist slitter, this one. And, yep, another failure." He turned back to me. "Hey, which way did you cut, pal? Across or up-and-down? I bet you did it across, yeah? Rarely works."

I had cut across my wrists but didn't answer.

"Leave off," the nurse said. "The last thing he needs is your advice."

"Well, half these suicides aren't serious, are they? It doesn't take much research to find out how to do the job right. He's probably just another one of them attention seekers, wouldn't you say?" He addressed the other patient. "You know all about that, don't you, pal?"

"You keep this up," the nurse warned, "and I'll get you shifted to a ward where no-one will listen to you."

He sniffed. "What's for breakfast? Same old shit?" He rose and sat on the edge of his bed.

"Oh, you're such a grateful sod, aren't you? Get up. Don't you know I report everything you say to the Doc?"

"Well, tell him I want to leave. I'm ready for a discharge. He doesn't listen to me. But you know I'm ready, right, sweetheart?"

The nurse put her hands on her hips, cocked her head, and studied him for a moment. The smile she wore suggested she knew this was a game. "And how long do you think it'd be before you're back in here?"

A book hit the wall near my bed and flopped to the floor like a dead fish. He suspended his arm in the air in a histrionic gesture. "It's a shit read!"

"Now cut it out, love. I'm serious! Show some respect."

"Respect? No cunt's ever shown me any."

"Well, go and have your breakfast anyway."

Breakfast was in an adjacent room. The nurse helped me out of bed and into a dressing gown. When she offered to put my broken arm in a sling, I declined. I had slippers in the side cupboard.

"Where am I?" I asked.

"It's hospital, love." She told me the name of the same hospital where I had been with my broken arm. I had heard of its psychiatric wing but understood it was for lunatics.

Once my gratuitous advisor had left, the other two patients started to stir. The nurse led me into the makeshift dining room where a gathering of the inhabitants of other wards, some dressed, some still in pyjamas, male and female, helped themselves to cereal and toast and coffee or tea and sat to eat at steel tables. One or two kept up incoherent patter; the rest were silent. I couldn't eat but had a cup of tea. Some patients were already playing pool at a table near a secured emergency exit door.

Later I sat on the edge of my bed, trying to ignore my antagonist carping about his treatment and his internment and being ignored by the medical staff. My wrists were sore and my gut felt like it had been wrung brutally to squeeze every drop of fluid from it. When the nurse returned, I asked her who had brought me here, and she explained I had arrived in an ambulance, but my mother and sister had come soon after.

"You've been under sedation twenty-four hours," she said as she packed up some monitoring equipment. "You needed quite a bit of blood. Is your belly sore?"

"Yeah."

"You had to have a stomach pump. You're one of the lucky ones. You know, whatever it is that made you do this, wasn't worth it, love. In no time at all you'll be glad you're here and not in a box." She looked around to check no other staff was listening, cautious about to give me some advice that fell outside her job description. "Life's precious. I know. I have moments when I've felt bad, but something always comes along, and it might only be something really small, hardly noticeable, and it'll make you realise you're glad to be alive. It might be something like flowers or a little kid walking for the first time. Something as simple as that can make it all worthwhile. You'll see, love, you'll see."

She gave me an affectionate punch on the arm, apparently forgetting it had been broken. I tried not to wince.

"Come on, get dressed. Your stuff is in the cupboard over there. And go back into the rec room. Did you notice the pool table? Have a game with some of the others. Most of them are nice. They'll like you, too, I'm sure. Go on."

So I went and met Melancholy, who was waiting for someone to play against. She told me that was her name, although it was probably Melanie. A dour teenager a bit older than me with long, straight, mousy hair, no makeup, and rings through her nose and bottom lip, she said nothing, just motioned with her head towards the pool table. Tosh had one in our games room, but I had never learnt to play properly because of his impatience and his competitiveness and his compulsion to ridicule almost every shot I made, accusing me of playing like a poofter, trying to belittle me, which he explained, when I complained, was all part of the game. "It's called sledging, pal, get used to it." It was a term I had only ever heard in relation to cricket.

Melancholy handed me a cue.

"I don't play much," I said, hesitating. "I'm not too good at it."

She was already setting up the triangle, taking little notice of my excuse. "Suits me." She set the white ball up. "You want to break?"

I shook my head and she did the honours, sinking three balls before I had a turn. Fortunately, I used my broken arm just to guide the cue, or I wouldn't have been able to play at all. My shot was fairly straightforward, but it hit the side of the cup and bounced out.

"I can see why you're in here," she said, nodding towards my bandages. "Wanna hear my excuse?"

I wasn't sure I wanted to know what her problem was, but she told me before I had a chance to answer. "I'm schizo, like most of the dudes in here. I got voices inside my head,"—she pointed to her temple with the chalking end of her cue— "telling me to kill people."

Her smile was defiant. "You're not scared, are you?"

I didn't know what to say, so I shrugged, which seemed to satisfy her. She resumed playing, expressionless, a study in concentration, and won the game. "Wanna play again?" she asked, already setting up the triangle.

It didn't worry her that I was no good at it. Nor did she brag about winning. We played for most of the morning until the nurses directed us back to our beds for routine medical check-ups and medication. The doctor doing the rounds asked me how I was feeling and I said, apart from feeling like crap, I felt okay.

When I sat next to Melancholy at lunch she began to tell me about her boyfriend who had overdosed on a drug he thought was Ecstasy. They had gone to a rave party in a warehouse at a derelict wharf on the Yarra River. She had been with him in the ambulance when he died on the way to hospital. He was the love of her life and the grief she suffered had been the catalyst for her mental illness. The medics had to restrain her from pummelling his corpse. He had abandoned her. She was hospitalised immediately and when she was discharged she tried to join him as she put it, failed, was hospitalised again, where she began to hear voices telling her how useless and cowardly she was, warning her that friends and family were conspiring against her to stop the 'reunion' occurring. She looked at me, expecting me to comment. I wracked my brain for something positive to say, eventually settling for, "I wish I was as good as you at pool."

"Do you want to fuck me?" she said.

Startled, I couldn't find the words to respond. So I nodded.

"I do it with anyone these days," she added and wrote a phone number in biro on one of my the bandages. "When we're out of here, give me a call. We'll shoot some pool first."

I watched her leave the table. She had an appointment with the resident psychiatrist. I ogled her bum and thighs as she walked away and had an anticipatory erection before she reached the nurses' station.

My appointment with the psychiatrist was later in the day. He was ancient, with a narrow, dimpled chin and elongated nose at the end of which sat a tiny pair of glasses. His thick, damp lips pursed as he observed me in silence. I sat in discomfort on a leather cushioned chair, looking at the certificates on the wall and a portrait of someone in a kilt, anywhere but into his gaze.

When the silence began to feel oppressive, he cleared his throat. "Tell me about yourself," he muttered in a rich Scottish brogue. "Why do you think you're here, in this hospital?"

I thought the answer was obvious, but from my former research, in Damien's home library, I learned that shrinks were only interested in sex. More silence ensued.

Eventually, he tried a different tack. "You come from a good family I hear, and a good clan, by the way, the McIntoshes." He chuckled warmly, glanced at the figure in the kilt, trying to charm me into an allegiance.

"That's a matter of opinion," I retorted.

"Go on."

I indulged him, spending half an hour telling him about what a great father I had.

When I finally stopped, he sighed. "So, are you doing anything that might be upsetting him?"

"Upsetting him?" I whined. "He's upsetting me."

"Yes, but what about your own recent activities?"

I shook my head in dismay. "He shits me."

"Answer me honestly, Alan. Are you using drugs at the moment? Whatever you say will go no further than this office."

"He's been talking to you, hasn't he?"

"Your father is extremely concerned about you, as any parent would be if their child had acted as you have. This animosity you feel towards him is really envy, isn't it? It's not unusual in young men. Most overcome it and reach a point where they reconcile, even love, their fathers. Others, well, a minority let it fester. Do you understand where I'm going with this?"

"That's just Freudian bullshit," I replied, again thanks to Damien's home library. "Oedipus, or something."

He seemed surprised. He sniffed.

"You strike me as in intelligent young fellow. Why don't you put your intelligence to good use? Keep off the drugs before they enslave you. Marijuana is just the start."

"Tosher's got a big mouth."

"Who? Oh, I see, McIntosh," he guessed accurately.

"What's he been telling you?" I insisted.

The old Scotsman squinted at me. "Next it will be methamphetamines or heroin."

I tried mockery. "So I should give up the dope and stick with the whiskey, should I, like a good Scot?"

"Don't waste that gift you've got, young man. Your intelligence. Soon you'll be able to go home, and my advice to you is to reconcile your differences. Your father is a decent fellow, a hard-working businessman."

"You haven't been listening to me, have you?"

"There's just one other matter, Alan. One of my other patients informed me you've been pestering her for sex."

"What?"

He pointed to my bandage. On impulse, I pulled my arm away, which appeared like an admission of guilt.

"Whose number is that?" he enquired.

The penny dropped. "She wrote it. I didn't ask for it."

"Well, if you say so. Do you like her?"

"She's all right."

"If you like her, the best thing you can do for her is leave her be."

After I left the wise psychiatrist, I went looking for Melancholy, but she was nowhere to be found. I asked the nurse.

"She's gone," she said.

I tried to phone her but got no response. I tried again later in the day. An irate male voice answered. "What do you want?"

"I thought this was Melancholy's number."

"Who?"

"I don't know—Melancholy?"

"If you blokes keep hassling her, I'll get the cops onto you. Don't call again." The phone went dead.

The bandages were removed and replaced before I had a chance to write the number down. Paranoid about another encounter with the cops, I wasn't entirely disappointed. I'd felt a connection to Melancholy but the serendipitous moment had passed. I never saw her again.

A couple of days later I went home in a taxi. I didn't set eyes on Tosh for days. There was a crisis with his franchises demanding his entire attention.

11

Tosh always wanted to be his own boss and perhaps he might have started a butcher's shop, a profitable business in my grandparents' day when local shopping strips were still viable and the price of meat was cheap, apparently. But the first sign of his business acumen surfaced when he realised he could never compete with the supermarkets. Most of the butchers he knew were accepting their fate and going to work for one or other of the two big chains. But not Ray McIntosh. He wasn't going to be anyone's hireling. Instead, he abandoned his trade and opted for a fast food franchise. The second sign was finding an accountant who hated the Tax Department as much as he did, who measured his professional worth with every cent he kept from its coffers.

When Tosh first went into business I was too young to be interested in what he did. I vaguely remember the stifling atmosphere, the unpleasant odours and the brown and yellow decor of his chicken outlet, the couple of times my mother took me there, which matched his work gear and the odours he brought home each night. In the early days he participated in preparation, customer service, and even clean-up after hours. It was only after he acquired his second outlet he assumed a more executive role and employed a couple of men to oversee the daily grind, although he had no real inclination or idea how to delegate. Apparently he had invested in other enterprises and schemes I hadn't heard about as well.

It was greed that led him to expand his business. He wasn't satisfied with the success he made of one outlet, which provided us with a comfortable standard of living. He wanted to attain the affluence of those rags-to-riches moguls who were always declaring on TV and in magazine articles that if they could make it, anyone could, it just required ambition and a lot of hard work, which was a way of saying they deserved more praise and admiration than those who inherited wealth and those who had none but hadn't (and never would) reach their heights due to a welfare mentality or downright indolence. To establish a second chicken outlet, a problem emerged when the banks refused his loan applications, with a warning he was overcommitting financially and would be in danger of defaulting on his current loans. So Tosh had to borrow heavily from unorthodox sources that demanded higher interest rates. As a result he was relying on the canny accountant to juggle his books and minimise the tax burden he faced. It put his mind at ease. He was able to present an easy-going, confident persona to the world, until he received notification from the tax office that he and his accountant were under investigation. It destroyed his composure, aged him overnight. His hair started to turn grey.

Around this time he caught me smoking marijuana, and then my initial contact with the police department and my suicide attempt prompted him to take drastic action. He gathered up our camping gear, which we he had acquired long ago but rarely used, bought supplies and took me into the wilderness for my own private boot camp, although, later, I suspected he wanted time out from the mess he had made of his business.

At last finding a proper use for his SUV, Tosh instructed me to load our camping gear, which included three plastic drums of water, indicating to me, when he refused to reveal our destination, that we were heading inland into arid country. He left the city via the Calder Highway—

complaining about the surface condition of the road, which I reminded him required more taxes to pay for any upgrade—minimizing talk with a few grunts at my enquiries about our trip, listening at first to a nostalgia radio station and then to one Rolling Stones CD after another. It took us three days to reach the vast salt pan, Lake Eyre, which every ten years or so fills with water after some rare weather occurrence in the Gulf country to the north, creating a profusion of life. But when we arrived, after staying in motels for two nights on the way, the only living creature I saw—besides Tosh, who looked barely alive from the ordeal of driving over hostile terrain—was an emaciated dog, maybe a dingo, slinking away in the distance. There were no birds in the sky, no livestock, no vegetation offering shade. The sunlight was cruel, depriving objects in the landscape of clear definition. My eyelids closed involuntarily. Sunglasses did little to reduce the glare. I had never seen such pure white as the salt pan. Ubiquitous and unavoidable, it was painful to view.

"Unload the gear," he said.

"We'll die out here."

"We've got enough water for a week."

I left the Land Cruiser and immediately felt the heat through my runners. "Fuck!"

"I won't have you using foul language out here. Unload the gear."

"By myself?"

"You'll be doing everything by yourself for both of us. Cooking, serving the meals, washing up afterwards, keeping the campsite clean, digging a latrine, you name it, you're doing it."

"And the rest of the day?" I jested bitterly. "I don't like our chances of catching fish out here. We should've just gone to Station Pier. We'd be home by dinner time."

He ignored my feeble joke. "We'll be talking. I'll be asking questions. You'll be answering. And then you'll be listening to me."

"We could've done that at home. Why'd you bring me way out here? There's just nothing here."

"It's a special place."

"Special because there's nothing here?"

"This's where Donald Campbell broke the world speed record in the Bluebird back on the seventeenth of July, nineteen-sixty-four, on my tenth birthday. Fastest man on Earth. You know what that did for me? Taught me the biggest lesson of my life. A man can do anything if he puts his mind to it, and puts his heart and soul into it. It's called ambition, buddy, and that's something you've never understood."

"Big difference between breaking world speed records and selling roast chicken," I suggested.

"Tell me that in ten years' time, once you see how I've developed my business, and you won't be so smug. And you could be a part of my team, if you want."

It was late afternoon. I was wearing a T-shirt, shorts and a cotton hat with a narrow brim that did little to protect me from the sun. Rivulets of sweat were rolling down my neck. The last thing I felt like doing was talk to Tosh. "I bet—what's his name, Campbell?—I bet he didn't have to camp in a swag while he was out here," I muttered.

"Don't be a smart-arse. All I've ever wanted of you is to show a bit of ambition. I've tried to get you interested in this and that over the years—nothing! I put you in a school that brings out the best in its scholars."

"Students."

"Scholars! That's what the school—the teachers, the principal, the brochure—called yous, for a reason. You weren't just students."

"They were wankers."

"What a waste of bloody money that was! And how did you repay me for all my efforts?"

He eloquently enumerated all my sins in case I had forgotten them. "I mean, fuck, Alan, this is a crisis, and crisises call for drastic action, which is why we're here."

"It's *crises*. The plural is *crises* , not *crisises*."

"Well, I'm glad your expensive education wasn't a total waste."

I was close to tears. "So, you're caring, are you? That's why you came to see me at the hospital, I suppose."

He called me a smart-arse once more and reminded me of how busy he had been to keep the family afloat, what, with all the government red tape, the price of everything, including my medical bills and that I was the most ungrateful sod he'd ever met, to which I responded with my own list of grievances. I couldn't prevent the tears from coming. The floodgates opened and I bawled until snot dripped from my nose.

My grief made him uneasy. "All I've ever wanted from you is a bit of respect and all I've ever wanted you to be is a successful young man. What's wrong with that? It's what every father wants for his son."

"I'm not interested in success," I cried, my voice rising in despair.

"What's wrong with success, for fuck's sake? My success in business is why you've got such an easy life today, my boy. All my hard work. And what do I get for a son? A dope-smoking, bludging wimp, who's got nothing better to do than cut his wrists. I won't put up with it. Not without trying to do something to straighten you out. That's why we're out here."

"How's that going to work?" I exaggerated my incredulity, waving my arms about.

"Well, it's going to start by you unloading the Cruiser!"

He refused to help.

I wiped the snot from my lip and deposited it on the crystalline ground. I used the back of my hand to wipe away a few remnant tears and began the chores.

We had swags instead of a tent. He wanted us to sleep under the stars like a couple of jackeroos. I had to unload them with the rest of the camping gear: a portable stove, a couple of gas bottles, a gas light, cooking and eating utensils, food supplies, a fold-up table and chairs, a shovel to dig a latrine. The water containers stayed in the back of the vehicle. They were too heavy to lift out. I began to empty the first one, drinking a litre, afraid I was dehydrating. When I suggested he have some, Tosh refused, presumably because he thought it would look like a sign of weakness.

"What are we going to do out here?" I asked again.

"Discuss your future."

"The one I want or the one you want?"

He sat on a chair and lit a cigarette without responding. The sun began to subside. The temperature dropped. The glare softened enough to remove my sunglasses. I opened a couple of cans of beans and heated them in a pot on the stove. We ate in a realm of silence that extended to the setting sun. When he had finished his meal he went to the

Cruiser, took something from the glovebox, returned to his chair and pointed at the lake. "Take a look at that." And while he thought I was distracted by the salt turning pink in the sunset he swigged from a flask.

"Can I have some?"

I thought I saw hatred in his eyes as they darted in my direction as if I had accused him of hypocrisy. "We didn't come all this way for a party," he said, wiping his lips with his forearm. "You're out here to straighten out. If you paid more attention to your surroundings, it might be a start."

"And you're leading by example, I suppose."

"How many fucking times do I have to warn you?"

"You also warned me about swearing. But you're doing more of that than I am."

"Is that so?" he jeered, jutting his head forward. He got to his feet. It was so quiet on the salt pan I heard his knees creak. He took a couple of steps towards me, trying to display his authority. So I stood as well in a pointless attempt to negate it.

"I'll decide what's being said and what's not round here. And, if you don't listen up, I'll get right back in the Cruiser," and his hand went out to point a finger at the vehicle, which was creaking like his knees as it cooled. "I'll fucking leave you out here on your own. See how smart you are then. I've put up with your nonsense long enough, boy, and it's going to stop right here, right now."

It seemed like a good idea to me. I matched his withering stare with a defiant one. In the minute that passed I didn't avert my eyes once, and he had to accept his plan for me was doomed. He lifted the flask to his lips and took an indulgent draught, his eyes on me all the while, before turning away.

After he returned to his camp chair he screwed the top onto the flask but clung to it like a prayer book. He looked exhausted. His eyelids drooped and so did his mouth. He sniffed loudly and returned his gaze to the lake where the pink hue was fading to blue. I waited for him to continue his harangue but his eyelids shut. And after a minute or two I realised he had fallen asleep. I took my eating utensils, collected his from the ground and washed them in cold water before I climbed into my swag next to the Cruiser. The temperature kept dropping. A myriad stars peppered the darkness, each one a sun with possible planets and life like on Earth, ready to remind me of my own insignificance. I wondered if any of them had life resembling humans. I hoped not. I was deep in introspection when I heard Tosh fall from his chair, gasp and grunt, pick himself up, muttering, cursing, stumbling around looking for his swag.

I must have slept for a few hours because, when I suddenly awoke, the moon in the shape and colour of a cantaloupe was directly overhead. I mistook it for the light in my bedroom. What woke me was a scream. I heard wailing followed by panicky breathing, a car door opening, banging, cursing, muttering.

"Get up! Let's get out of here!" Tosh was next to me, hauling me up in my swag.

"What? What's happening?"

"Get in the fucking car!"

His panic was infectious. I struggled out of the swag and rushed for the passenger seat suspecting we were under attack from aliens, or desert Aborigines, or post-apocalyptic feral white men. Tosh leapt into the driver's seat and we were accelerating across the salt pan, in emulation of Donald Campbell, before I had time to put on my seat belt.

"What's going on?" I demanded in a frightened voice.

Tosh didn't answer. He was trying to control the vehicle as he sped into the unknown, his head extended towards the windscreen, trying to improve his vision, his mouth agape, emitting strangled noises. He turned the vehicle's fog lights on, attempting to recreate daylight, casting a bleak glare across the nothingness outside.

"Do you know where you're going?" I asked after five minutes, when nothing catastrophic had descended upon us.

"There's a track here somewhere," he muttered.

Miraculously some ruts appeared in the lights and he decided to follow those. They could have been our own tracks but he wouldn't countenance the possibility that he was driving around in circles. A half hour passed and the ruts seemed to be mutating into a road of sorts. There were signs at the edges that a grader had passed by, perhaps years earlier.

"Are you going to tell me what happened back there?"

"You don't want to know."

"You're shitting yourself." I was still nervous too. The adrenalin was flowing. But Tosh's fear was something to behold. For the first time in my life I felt less scared, less weak, than he was.

"Something got into my swag," he blurted. "Woke me up. I didn't know what it was. And there was something else."

"What?"

I waited but he seemed reluctant to answer.

"A presence," he muttered eventually.

"A what?"

"A presence. Something, someone, nearby. We were in danger, Al. I had to get us out of there."

"What do you think it was, a spook?"

"I don't know. Maybe." The road was gaining definition. Tosh began to calm down a little. "Maybe an Abo."

"And what was in your swag?"

"I don't know. A snake? Maybe he put a snake in me swag."

I looked over my shoulder at the storage area. "Then it's probably in the car," I muttered.

"I left it behind."

"What, the snake?"

"The swag."

I looked again and realised most of our camping gear had been abandoned. "Didn't you pack up our stuff?"

"We were in danger, Al. I've saved your life, you realise."

Under his fringe, his glance was trying to assess if I believed him. He sniffed back his disappointment.

I returned my gaze to the road. It was still dark but away to the east there was the glimmer of dawn on the horizon. I stared at the ruts we were following, barely able to accept the significance of what I was hearing. Tosh had been terrified. He was human, after all. More than human, he was as much a coward as I was. Maybe a bigger one. I felt light-headed, almost elated.

"We should go back and get it," I counselled.

"We're not going back."

"We've got to. You paid big bucks for it, I bet"

"He can have it."

"Who?"

"The Abo."

"You're scared of the natives?" I raised my eyebrows and stared at him. "I thought you thought they were useless bludgers? Wouldn't work in an iron lung?"

He glanced at me sheepishly. "I'm not scared. It's just—you upset an Abo, you never know what he might do."

"Like put a snake in your swag?" I laughed. "Come on!"

"Like point the bone at you. I've heard they'll do that. Once that happens, it's curtains."

"And you believe that stuff?"

"All I was trying to do was protect you, son. If I'd have died, what would've happened to you? I had to get us out of there real quick. You should be thanking me."

"Faster than Donald Campbell," I sniggered. "Last night you were threatening to leave me out here on my own."

"That was talk."

"Ah, so all the rush—leaving all our gear behind—all that was for me, was it? Just like when you used to scare me as a kid. It was all for me, right? Well, I say, let's go back and get it. I don't reckon there was anybody there. You just got spooked by the wind or something. And our stuff will be just sitting there. If we don't, it'll stay there for God-knows-how-long, turning into junk."

"I don't know where we were."

The sun emerged. An eerie light spread across the land. We were travelling across a stony plane devoid of vegetation. We might as well have been on the moon.

"Abo land," he murmured. "It gives me the creeps."

"Then the whole country must give you the creeps."

He didn't look at me but I noticed the muscles in his jaw and neck tighten. "It's not all Abo land," he muttered and hit a knob on the audio system. Suddenly there was ululation—from Mick Jagger—from our civilization.

12

Tosh blamed me for the debacle. If I hadn't been a wayward son we would never have been in the place that caused his panic attack. There was only one thing I could do to redress the humiliation I had inflicted. I had to work for him at one of his chicken joints. "Get a taste of how the other half lives and you might appreciate what I've done for you over the years." He jutted his chin doggedly. "And you'll see how hard your father works."

"And who's he?"

He raised his hand, but checked his impulse to swipe me as I ducked away. "You never learn, do you?" he snarled.

"I think I have. I was ready for you."

I resisted his generous employment offer. I shaved off all my hair, with clippers first and then the shaver he'd bought me. I stared at my image in the bathroom mirror. A convict or an inmate from a lunatic asylum stared back. He was gaunt and pallid. His eyes were intense. He appeared famished, not the sort of employee that a customer would wish to encounter. Even I was startled. I rubbed my scalp to see if the reflection copied my movement, so uncertain was I of its provenance. It imitated me. It sneered when I did. I nodded resolutely. I was certain Tosh would realise I was unsuitable for his outlets. Pleasing, too, was the absence of an imposing fringe, which meant I no longer looked anything like him.

As soon as Tosh saw me, he understood my motive. "That's not going to get you out of this," he jeered.

He found a cap with a chicken insignia and slapped it on my head. "Wear that." He pulled it down tight. "And don't take it off."

"I don't think I can," I quipped.

He wouldn't give me a lift to the outlet, even when he was going there. A thirty-minute trip in a car took an hour and twenty minutes on public transport. Another lesson I had to learn, apparently.

Because of my appearance I was kept away from customers. I worked in the kitchen, cooking and dispensing fries as the orders came in. The work was hot and greasy. There was a repugnant smell about the food that put me off eating chicken for the rest of my life. But the worst aspect of the job was the way the other employees tried to ingratiate themselves to Tosh whenever he was around. They were young, poorly-paid casuals who considered fawning necessary in order to keep their jobs. When they discovered I was the boss's son they were courteous but wary of me, avoiding me during scheduled breaks and on the buses I took, limiting their conversation when they were rostered to work beside me, always cautious lest I be the company spy, or perhaps because I looked crazy. For my part I couldn't care less whether they liked me or not. I gave them no reason to dislike me aside from being related to their exploiter—sorry, that's Patrick's influence—employer—whom I avoided at work, and I let them know with my silence and sullenness that I hated the job and was only there under duress.

Most of the time Tosh wasn't around. Matt Harrison was the manager of the outlet where I worked. But manager was a misnomer. He was really an overseer, like a galley master or head chef, who took orders from a redoubtable proprietor. Sinewy, like a refugee from Famineland and wearing a cook's cap with the company logo over his thinning hair, he lingered in the kitchen looking at the food with wistful scavenger's eyes. But no-one could accuse him of eating the profits. He forbad employees consuming anything off the menu while on the job, not even leftovers at the end of the night. If they wanted chicken or fries, they would have to buy them like any other customer. And he led by example, obeyed his own rules, although I think, like me, he had an aversion to greasy food and was never tempted. Leftovers came home with Tosh, if he was around, but I refused to eat them.

Harrison had a way of issuing instructions as questions, which used to annoy me, but no doubt he thought it was an astute managerial technique, something he had learnt from one of those leadership manuals or picked up at an entrepreneurial seminar. Even more annoying was his habit of leaving glossy cards with biblical quotations on shelves and tables throughout the building, proselytizing on the sly for the evangelical church he attended. "Alan, why don't you take a cloth and wipe down the tables?" he ordered one evening when there were few customers inside. "Can you pick up any rubbish, too?"

I collected the cards I found on the tables and waved them before his eyes. "Are these rubbish?" I asked in my most innocent voice. "Looks like it."

He pretended not to hear me.

"I'll take that as a *yes*, then, will I? I mean, what sort of idiot would leave nonsense like this lying around?"

Perhaps he feared I might tell Tosh if he insisted they remain where he had put them. But I had no intention of reporting him. I couldn't have cared less. I just wanted him to know what I thought of his sneakiness.

If there was anything positive about the job, it was getting regular pay. I no longer had to beg my mother for extra cash over and above the spare change I stole from purses and pockets and the stingy fortnightly allowance I received from Tosh, which used to last about three days. One night travelling home on the bus I saw my old dealer sitting in his car near a park in our neighbourhood. I got off at the next stop and sauntered back.

I started to smoke heavily again. Although I preferred bongs, I always started my day with a joint and a cup of coffee from a stall near the railway station. With the old widow's shed off limits I had to find a new place to consume my morning start-up. The railway crossed a creek a couple of hundred metres from the station and there were bushes either side of its bridge that lent me some privacy. There was even a place up high in the brick structure where I could hide my bong and the bottle of whiskey I still occasionally pilfered, these days from bottle shops rather than Tosh's cellar. I became adept at overriding the store security exits, something I was proud of. By the time I reached school I was off my face, always late, for which I received detention, which was neither here nor there to me and merely enhanced my reputation as a singular, solitary dude who didn't give a fuck about anything, an attitude I believed most other students envied, even respected, but were too insecure to emulate. The illusion was all mine of course. I was lonely and more insecure than they were and too self-conscious to try to make friends, given my only real friends, Jonathan and Damien, had deserted me for no reason I could understand.

I had tried to phone and text them but they hadn't responded. I even went around to Damien's place in Parkville but was greeted by his aunt who told me I was *persona non grata*. When I asked her why, she said it was not for her to go into the details.

"This is Kafkaesque," I told her, using one of The Damaged Sons Club's favourite expressions. "Tell Damien that, will you?"

I was in my final year of high school. I had refused to do the subjects Tosh insisted I do: maths, economics, and commerce. Instead I had enrolled in the humanities: literature, art, history of revolutions, and one of the languages that was on offer at the school, Mandarin, of which I learnt little more than *ni hao*, my class attendance was so poor. The only other student at the school I had spoken to in anything other than an English monosyllable was Sky, and she had disappeared into child-protectionland. My consumption of weed increased. I was smoking joints before school, joints during my lunchbreak and bongs after school. Before I entered the chicken outlet for work in the evenings, I smoked another joint. After work, ditto. The drug was costing me so much I was stealing what money I could from my parents again. I pleaded with my mother for an access card into one of her accounts, but she refused.

Towards the end of the year I was stoned most of the day. My studies suffered. The covert diligence of my first months at the school had gradually slackened. Teachers started pressuring me to drop out so that my anticipated poor results wouldn't drag down their averages. Reputations were at stake here. The principal summoned me to her office, made sure of our privacy, and then told me what a piece of shit she thought I was, just like the hospital psychiatrist had done, except a little more directly. She knew about my drug habit. She knew my father was a decent, hard-working businessman, who shouldn't have to endure the damage I inflicted on our family's reputation, because if I thought my antisocial behaviour didn't reflect on the whole family, I was more stupid and solipsistic than she imagined. (When I looked up *solipsistic* in the dictionary afterwards I thought it pretty much summed up my attitude.) But what concerned her more than my family's reputation was the school's reputation, built over the years on solid academic results and the low incidence of delinquency, which ranked it amongst the top ten of desirable government schools in the state and either I started putting some serious effort into my studies or she would find a way of getting rid of me.

So I made it easy for her.

Tosh got wind of my notoriety. He must have paid someone to follow me. One morning, as I was reclining on the slope beneath the railway bridge, a photographer appeared and took a few snaps of me lying on an old blanket with a joint in one hand, a coffee in the other, and my dope paraphernalia, including the bong, at my side. He was gone before I had a chance to react. It was either the local paper chasing a cover story for its campaign to convince the readership they were living in the most dangerous suburb on earth, in the hope of increasing the paper's dwindling circulation, or else the principal was bulking out my dossier, gathering the evidence she needed to expel me. It didn't cross my mind that it might have been Tosh until he burst into my room the following Saturday morning, waving the photos like some lucky punter down at the betting agency with his winning trifecta ticket, while I was still in bed enjoying a languid wank. "You're still at it!" he yelled and I thought he meant the masturbation. So I pulled my hands from under the bedclothes and raised them like a cornered fugitive. He tossed the photos on the bed but I didn't have to view them to know what they were about.

"You pay someone to spy on your own son!" I cried, trying futilely to gain the upper moral ground.

"That's because you need spying on. I shouldn't have wasted me time and money taking you to Lake Eyre, thinking I could talk some sense into you."

"Oh, yeah, a lot of sense you talked out there."

Before I could defend myself he grabbed the front of my pyjamas and hoisted my head and shoulders off the pillow with one hand while he slapped my head backwards and forwards with the other as if he were trying to wake me from a swoon.

My ears rang. My cheeks burned. I fell back onto the pillow and guessed his assault was over. I wanted him to think I had become immune to his violence. So I grinned at him, the wrong response I soon discovered. He changed colour faster than a chameleon. His face and neck glowed a rude cerise. His eyes became incandescent. He grabbed me again, this time with two hands, and hoisted me from the bed, hurled me to the floor and began to kick, until I curled up to protect myself.

"I went and found your little hideout with the bong and the packet of dope and that bottle of whiskey, which wasn't one of mine so you must've stole it from somewhere else."

"I didn't steal it," I lied. "I bought it."

"You couldn't have bought it. You're still under age."

I looked at him through my fingers, which were protecting my head. "God, you're naive," I blurted, which did earn me another kick, this time in the backside.

In reflex I lost my defensive posture, allowing him to grab my pyjamas by the lapels and hurl me to my feet. I heard the material rip.

"I wished you'd never been born," he jeered, spraying me with his rancid, moist, nicotine breath. "I wished I had another son, a decent son who respected me, who appreciated what I do for him. You, you're just a waste of space."

He let go and I collapsed to the floor.

Then I heard an alarming sound. A sob. Was he crying? He turned away.

"I've clocked your dealer, too," he croaked, "and given his plate number to the police."

"You shouldn't have done that."

"Done it. So he'll be taken off the street."

I groaned.

"I was going to kick you out. You don't deserve to live here. But your mother talked me out of it." His voice was still quavering; I was astonished to witness his sensibility. "You can thank her you won't be sleeping on the street tonight. Instead I'm going to double your working hours so you've got less spare time on your hands, and hope that teaches you how to act like a normal human being."

"Like you, you mean?" I muttered, but he was gone.

He left me crumpled on the floor where I stayed for the next half hour, feeling woeful, reflecting on how alone I was. I had no-one to turn to. My friends had deserted me for reasons I didn't understand. My family was ashamed of me, even my sister, who considered me weak-willed and anti-social and a drag on her own personal appeal, the gorgeous chick with the really weird brother—a stigma she would prefer to live without—even my mother, who considered me a drain on her purse, the cause of all the tension within the family, and the son she couldn't boast about in her social circle. My sense of isolation was acute.

The idea of leaving, of becoming homeless, crossed my mind. But to be honest it scared me, more than Tosh's beatings. I had seen homeless people around the city and realised there was no coming back once you were on the streets; it was an endless spiral downwards.

The thought of suicide occurred again but after my last humiliating effort it had lost most of its appeal. Education seemed my only viable escape route. The plan to reunite with Damien and Jonathan at university still held some purchase on my feeble mind. With only a couple of months to the end of the year, every time the final exams intruded unpleasantly into my consciousness, panic and dread overwhelmed me. I hadn't done much of the course work, which meant I had to perform well above average in the exams. It was unlikely to happen. I blamed Tosh. I blamed the world for Tosh. If I failed my exams I had no idea what to do, except I was determined I wouldn't work for him. Every time my thoughts shifted to the future they whirled and crashed in on themselves. At times I hyperventilated.

Then Tosh had another brilliant idea, almost as inspired as our trip to Lake Eyre. I was to accompany him on an excursion to one of his suppliers. "Come and see how I do business." He rubbed his hands together and grinned. "Dead cert, boy, you'll change your mind about following in my footsteps once you see how I operate."

He was developing furrows down his cheeks thanks to the stress of dealing with a maverick son on top of running two franchises and trying to negotiate a third, the donut business in Chadstone Shopping Centre. At the slightest dissent or disagreement these furrows made the skin between look like subcutaneous tentacles trying to escape their containment beneath his greasy mop of hair. I grumbled and for a moment his head looked like a jelly fish.

"I'm asking you nicely. It's your choice, but if you don't come, you're out of my house," he warned agreeably. "You can go live under your bridge, for all I care." He stood in front of me, squeezed my shoulder, and offered me a dissembling smile.

I decided to accompany him.

"Wear your suit," he advised.

"I don't have one."

"The one we bought you." When I outgrew the suit I wore to the strip club, my mother had bought me another, once again for funerals.

I shrugged. "Gone." I had gotten rid of it, taken it to an op-shop and exchanged it for an old leather jacket I liked, which I put on instead.

He gaped at me, speechless, as if it had just occurred to him that I was incorrigible.

"It got lost at the dry cleaners," I added.

"Have you ever worn it?" he exclaimed. "What was it doing at the dry cleaners?"

I grimaced with faux sincerity. "Semen stains."

That seemed credible to him. "And did they compensate you for it?"

"Handsomely."

Since our farcical trip to the salt pan he leant forward over the steering wheel whenever he drove, as if he expected something diabolical to suddenly appear. His fringe fell forward, slightly away from his forehead. His mouth was open. The bottom lip hung loose. I watched him furtively from the front passenger seat, convinced we weren't related. This man was a total stranger to me. He must have been deluded if he thought I was his son. So why was he going to all this effort to demonstrate his business acumen? For the briefest of moments I felt sorry for him. Since he was driving and couldn't assault me without risking his own life, I tried once more to raise the matter. "I'm not your son," I said, offering him a release from the onerous task of bringing me up.

"What?"

"I'm not your son, so you don't have to do this."

We were heading out of the city, travelling south along an expressway through endless suburbs. He glanced across at me. "You've mentioned that once too often!"

"No, no, it's just occurred to me, like God was telling me, or something. I heard a voice."

"Since when have you ever believed in God?"

"Since just now when he told me you weren't my father."

He chuckled at my audacity and then he hissed.

"Maybe Mum screwed some other guy," I added. "I don't know."

"You filthy-minded little layabout, if I weren't driving, I'd knock your bloody teeth out."

"You've already done that, remember? Cost you a fortune." Silence followed for a few kilometres. "It'd be good for both of us, don't you reckon, if it's true? You wouldn't have to worry about me anymore and I wouldn't have to be around you. No offence, we've just got nothing in common."

"No offence? You listen to me. If you do anything—anything!—to embarrass me today you'll get your wish. You won't be my son anymore. You'll be dead."

Silence ensued until we reached an off-ramp. We were still in the suburbs but a long way from the centre of the city. "You'll be dead," he repeated as if the idea was gaining traction with him.

He drove along a road until we left the residential district and entered an industrial zone. He turned into a factory with billboards at its entrance depicting cartoon images of happy chickens marching to their execution and an arching sign overhead announcing Pridges Poultry. Security allowed us to pass once Tosh's appointment and identity were checked. We stopped in the visitors' parking lot, adjacent to the main office.

"What's this all about, anyway?" I asked, feeling uneasy.

"You'll see."

"I won't get out of the car unless you tell me what this is all about."

He glanced at me and suddenly he looked pleased, misinterpreting me resistance for interest. "I want these fuckers to reduce their price per unit. Our margins are getting squeezed so tight, if they don't blink I'll be squeezing the balls of my employees until they accept a salary cut."

"What about your female employees? You've got a few of them."

"I'll squeezed their balls too. Come see how your old man does business." His tone rose like a football coach trying to instil some enthusiasm into his players in a pre-match huddle. "Listen and learn, boy, listen and learn. Watch these bastards wriggle and squirm."

"Getting into poetry these days, are you?" I said.

"What're you talking about?"

"Never mind."

We waited at reception an inordinate time. As we sat on a vinyl settee, looking at glossy before-and-after posters of chickens, I could detect Tosh's indignation through the reappearance of the jellyfish. I dreaded the outburst that would surely follow the marketing director's arrival if Tosh's reaction to my dissent was anything to go by. But when she appeared, an elegant, middle-aged woman, Tosh was all smiles, dismissing her apology with a nonchalant gesture and introducing me as his ambitious son, eager to follow in his father's footsteps once I finished my MBA.

She turned to me with a professional smile. "How far into it are you, Alan?" she asked.

"I'm still at high school," I responded, averting my eyes and giving an exasperated grimace to indicate how I felt about my father's assertion.

"Well, would you like to have a look at our production line while your father and I do business, see for yourself what we do here?"

I nodded. Anything to get away from Tosh.

"Ok, I'll get Laura to call one of our supervisors to show you around," she said, pointing toward the receptionist.

I shrugged. "Suits me."

Tosh affected an ingratiating smile. "I wouldn't mind him staying with us," he interjected. "Learn the ropes, if you know what I mean."

"I'm afraid that won't be possible. You understand. Business protocols. Confidentiality and all that. Now off you go, young Alan. I'm sure you'll find it fascinating."

She ushered Tosh into an office.

The receptionist contacted the supervisor who arrived after a few minutes. Introducing himself as Bill, he tossed his head as if he had a crick in the neck.

Bill was an alcoholic, no doubt about it. I could smell the ethanol seeping from his pores before he got close enough to shake hands. And maybe he could smell me. He was in a white dust coat, fawn P-P trousers and white synthetic leather runners. His eyes scrutinized my grey stovepipe jeans, black T-shirt and leather jacket, and his face twitched. "Let's get you decked out, buddy." He took me into a locker room, gave me a similar white coat to his own and showed me a locker where I could hang my jacket.

The tour began in the yard behind the main building, where trucks carrying wire crates of poultry arrived from farms. The crates, each about the size of a large suitcase, were removed from the trucks with forklifts, and taken into a storeroom. Men in leather gloves and overalls loaded the crates onto rollers to be conveyed through a hole in the wall.

Bill began his tour-guide spiel but I was barely listening, shocked as I was by the vision of thousands of trapped hens, their white feathers pressed against the wire grids. "The boys here call this death row," he shouted to be heard above the machinery noises. "Over thirty thousand birds a day pass through that hole. Come on, I'll show you."

He led me through a heavy sliding door into a large room. The floor and walls were concrete. The conveyor crossed the room into a mesh compound, which looked like the exercise yard in a prison replete with inmates who were dressed in white overalls that were soiled from dust and shit, courtesy of the hens they were taking from the cages to hang by the legs on overhead shackles.

Each bird struggled for its life, flapping its wings, kicking its legs in the grasping hands of the labourers. Occasionally one hen flipped up high enough for its head to obstruct the motion of legs from crate to shackle. Inadvertently the head then slipped into the shackle instead of the legs, frustrating the labourer, who had no time to lever it out, but, cursing, jerked down hard, decapitating the hen, freeing the carcass to be hung correctly. There were eight labourers inside the compound.

"Each bloke hangs up about four thousand chooks a day." Bill watched them for a while with his hands on his hips, like a proud coach. Then he turned to me. "They're lucky to have a job. Most of the production line is mechanised. And one day this will be too. Come on, I'll show you the rest."

The conveyor with the shackled birds moved to another section of the room where it entered a large container. "Inside there the chooks pass an electric probe that stuns them. They come out the other side—come round here, see there?"

What I saw were headless birds emerging. "There's rotating blades in that machine. Very humane," Bill said proudly. "When I started here, some thirty years ago, all them throats were cut manually. Half a dozen of us blokes stood in a row with our knives, getting covered in blood. It was everywhere. Bloody messy, I tell you, excuse the pun. Didn't matter how much you washed afterwards you could never get rid of all of it, especially the smell. Made it hard to pull a bird I can tell you." He saw me frown. "A chick." Then he laughed at his poor choice of words, given our location. "A girlfriend," hc clarified.

The headless birds, dripping blood and jerking, travelled through a hole in the wall into another room where it was hot and steamy. I soon saw the reason. There were huge vats of boiling water, one in operation, into which the headless chickens, still shackled to the overhead conveyor, were dunked. "In the old days, any bird that missed getting its throat cut would be boiled alive," Bill informed me.

The purpose of the dunking was to loosen the feathers. Immediately afterwards the drenched birds passed into a plucking machine, which consisted of large rollers with rubber protrusions that he called *fingers*.

Amidst the horror and in the humidity, I was almost swooning.

"Let's go look at the machines that do the gutting," he said, his enthusiasm unconstrained.

"You have machines that do that too?"

"Yeah, come, take a look."

But I couldn't take any more. My heart was palpitating. I was feeling nauseous and contrite about all the chicken I had eaten over the years without a thought for its slaughter. Admittedly I hadn't eaten chicken since I started working for Tosh but that was due to kitchen smells and not some heightened awareness. It had always been just meat to me, never a slaughtered animal. Seeing these birds losing their lives upset me more than I had expected. I was shocked. I realised I had more affinity with them than with my family. I decided then and there to stop eating meat of any sort. I couldn't imagine watching a cow or a sheep or a pig getting slaughtered.

"Well, are you coming or not?" Bill called when he realised I wasn't following him.

"Not," I muttered and hastened away. I found my own way back to the locker room, retrieved my jacket, and left by an emergency exit.

Waiting by the car for Tosh, my palpitations became shivers. As my imagination recreated the life and death of a chicken, my shivers were soon sobbing spasms.

"What's the matter with you? What are you bawling about? Pull yourself together, for Chrissakes. You cry at the drop of a hat. What are you doing out here?" His eyebrows ascended beneath his fringe, in disdain or dismay or disbelief, I couldn't tell. "They told me you just walked off. I could've guessed you'd pull some stunt like that."

I tried to control my emotions, shrugging, keeping my head turned away. "It was boring," I lied.

"It don't matter if it's boring. We're doing business here. You've got to look interested. You think I'm not bored half the time?"

"Why do you do it then?"

He looked across the roof of the car at me with a furious pout. "Because, dickhead, it's what I do. I'm in business. We can't all sniff the roses every minute of the bloody day."

I got into the car without responding, and he followed. Five minutes after we left the plant, with the Rolling Stones filling the void, he smashed a hand against the steering wheel. "Thanks for asking!"

I nearly shat myself, my fragile nerves yet to recover from the slaughterhouse experience. "What?"

"You've got no bloody interest in the business at all, have you? I've given you ten minutes to ask me how it went, and it hasn't even crossed your mind, has it?"

"What?"

"They're ruthless, them bastards. They've got me by the balls." I could see the tentacles in his cheeks again. "They wouldn't move. I wasn't asking for much, just to phase in the increase over two years, give me time to absorb the cost, but no! That bitch, she might be a good looker but she drives a hard bargain like some ugly old cunt. Like a bloke, she is."

Again I failed to respond.

"You're not interested, are you?" He was still shouting but now he was taking his eyes off the road and staring at me like I was the cause of all his woes.

"You should get out of the business," I suggested. "It's cruel and disgusting."

"What?" He remembered he was driving and turned his attention momentarily back to the road, made some adjustments to his trajectory and turned back to me. "Are you going soft in the head? They're just fucking chickens."

I started to yell back. "I said it's cruel! You ought to see how they're treated. They come packed in these cages where they can hardly move. They get strung up by the legs. They're all struggling. Some of them get their heads ripped off. No-one gives a fuck. They give them an electric shock." On and on I went while Tosh gripped the wheel, his eyes oscillating between me and the expressway, interrupting me with his own shouts—"You think I haven't seen it? Of course I have! So what? They're just stupid chooks."—until I ended up accusing him of committing the equivalent of Nazi war crimes, one of the things I remembered studying at school, invoking the concentration camps and the millions of Jews who'd been conveyed into gas chambers. I suspected it was a ridiculous analogy but I was emotionally distraught.

When we got home I left the car without a word, but before I made it to the front door he told me to get ready for work.

"I'm not going."

"Yes, you are, boy. You fall off a horse, you get straight back on."

"What's that meant to mean?"

"You got squeamish with the chickens today. Deal with it."

"I told you I'm not going."

I'll never forget how his face went iridescent. There was the jelly fish, the mop of hair and tentacles beneath, floundering in a tempest. He rushed at me before I could open the door, grabbed my neck in a vicelike grip and pushed me inside. I tried to resist but he was too strong. As we passed along the passage he opened a cupboard with his other hand and pulled out a wheelie suitcase before he continued to march me to my room, with me shouting and cursing the whole time, trying to tell him he was hurting my neck. Momentarily, my mother appeared from the living room, no doubt wondering what the racket was all about, but when she detected Tosh's venom, she withdrew.

In my room he tossed the suitcase onto the bed and released me.

"Start packing!"

"What for?"

"You aren't living here anymore."

"Good," I said, but he didn't seem to hear me.

"You don't work, you get out of my house."

"It's not just your house. It's Mum's. It's ours."

"Who bought it? Who's up to his eyeballs in debt because of it? Who pays all the fucking bills?" He was almost screaming at me, bending towards me and pointing at the door, although I was not sure why. "Your sister, your mother—you—yous have paid for none of it, not a cent! So don't go telling me whose house it is!"

I headed for my wardrobe and began to remove shirts in a fury, intending to put them in the suitcase. I hurled them onto the bed and headed for my drawers to get some underwear and T-shirts.

"What're you doing?"

"Packing."

He charged at me. "Don't be a smart-arse! Get yourself ready for work!"

Now he was screaming and slapping me around the head. My ears stung and the room swirled. I was on the floor. I tried to look up at him standing over me but my vision was blurred.

"I want to see you at work within the hour or this'll seem like a bit of shadow boxing. I'll come down on you like a ton of bricks. You won't know what hit you, you wuss."

I lay on the floor until he left and then I lay there longer, perhaps thirty minutes, long enough to know I wouldn't get to work within the hour, long enough for my mother to put her head around the door and ask if I was all right? I said, "Fine." She offered to help and I ordered her away.

My neck and head were aching. One of my arms felt broken again but I was able to move it and realised the pain was muscular. None of this bothered me as much as Tosh's threat. The rage and anxiety I experienced caused me to hyperventilate. A vortex of thoughts kept me prostrate. Murder and suicide were there—of Tosh and me respectively—along with the slaughter of chickens and the desperate way they had struggled to survive while I watched and attempted to save none. I was culpable. We all were. We let it happen. We ate them without a thought for their lives, which were precious to them but not to us. When I struggled to my feet, I packed the shirts into the suitcase and collected underwear and socks and T-shirts, put them in the suitcase as well. Finally I collected my bong and dope from a hiding place and tucked them under the clothing, muttering all the time that I would correct this injustice. I would not let the slaughter of chickens go unpunished.

The bus was almost empty. I sat at the rear with my suitcase, making plans, considering various strategies. I stared out the window at the vehicles. Their drivers were all culpable. I stared at the pedestrians, walking along in the twilight. They were all culpable. The couple of other passengers seated passively in front of me and the silent bus driver were culpable. It was unbearable, this universal indifference. I had to make people aware of what they had done, were still doing, to chickens.

It was dark when the bus reached the stop a block from the outlet where Tosh had me working. I alighted and waited for the bus to continue. I placed the suitcase on the bench in the bus shelter, opened it and added the clothes I was wearing, except for my shoes. Naked, I walked to the outlet and entered through the staff door. The purpose of my nakedness was to draw attention to the chickens that had been denuded, plucked, and to make a point about our similarities. Gagging on the stench of burning flesh, I grabbed two yet-to-be-roasted corpses from a bench and strode into the customer area, holding them aloft without Matt Harrison or any of his underlings noticing.

I heard a shriek before I had a chance to start my speech on the theme of animal cruelty, followed by indignant cries. After all, it was a family restaurant as well as a drive-through takeaway joint and there were children present, some of whom had probably never seen a naked adolescent before. I'm fairly certain my message was lost to the sensation of my nudity. Perhaps I should have kept the underpants on. It was a hundred and twenty kilo prize fighter who tackled me to the floor, calling me a bloody pervert and a filthy bastard. I tried to shout out, "Save the chickens!" but he held me, face down and sat on my back, squeezing the breath out of me in a grunt. Harrison arrived in haste with a couple of spare company aprons, as parents tried to keep their curious children away. Three of the underlings covered me with the aprons and got me out of sight while Harrison contacted my father. With the gorilla off my body I was able to issue my plea. "Save the chickens! Save the chickens! Murderers! Assassins! I have seen them slaughtered! You're all responsible. Kids, don't eat the chickens!"

A CAT team arrived before Tosh, which was a blessing because I could guess what he would have done to me. Instead I received an injection and that was the last thing I remember about the evening.

13

I spent the next few months, drugged senseless, in a clinic run by Christians. I remember a chapel where I was taken each day along with the other lunatics to cleanse our souls. During the day I wandered around the grounds in a torpor, talking to no-one except myself, avoiding other residents and medical staff whenever possible, with a simple, singular refrain in my head. *I'm a poet.* Where I got that idea from I had no idea. I couldn't think of a single poem I had written but it didn't seem to matter. *I'm a poet. I'm a poet.* I clung to the refrain like a lifebuoy.

The doctor I saw told me I'd had a psychotic episode and diagnosed a bipolar disorder. They had found my drug paraphernalia amongst my clothes in the suitcase, and she blamed drug use rather than the slaughter of chickens for my illness. She put me on a low dose of lithium and other drugs called stabilizers, including sleeping tablets, instructing me to participate in the clinic's exercise regime, assuring me I would be back to *normal* (whatever that meant) in no time at all if I followed her advice. She also told me that praying each day would accelerate the healing. I didn't know at the time that Matt Harrison, the manager of the outlet where I had protested the slaughter of chickens, had urged Tosh to send me to the clinic run by his church.

Open your heart to Jesus and you'll be saved was the message I heard each day. *Submit to God's will.* My madness, apparently, was due the Devil, in which case, I deduced, the Devil was against the slaughter of chickens and all in favour of poetry.

That period of my life is a blur for me. When I was released I had nowhere else to go but to Tosh's place, which I now refused to call home. My mother was solicitous but also disappointed. She advised me to get a hobby, start a miniature figurine soldier collection or something, and join the Young Liberals or a church youth group to meet some decent people my own age. My sister advised me to keep away from drugs. Unlike her, I couldn't handle them. I didn't have a strong enough will. "Face it, Al, you go psycho once," she confided, "it'll happen again."

While I was in the clinic, the school year ended. I missed my exams and the opportunity to go to university, the point of which was solely to reunite with Damien and Jonathan. But at least the school was relieved. I hadn't jeopardised its ranking.

My temperament over the following months—no, years— was controlled by prescribed medication. I stayed away from cannabis although I occasionally had alcohol. The last thing I wanted was another psychotic episode. I hung around the house, unwilling to risk an incursion into the public domain, where something or someone might trigger my bad habits. While Tosh's swimming pool was being built I would sit in the games room, overlooking the back yard and watch the excavation. Why he was going ahead with the costly addition to our lifestyle while his business was in trouble I had no idea. The backhoe was shaped like a giant scorpion scouring the earth with its tail, depositing dirt and rock into a small tip tray. Later the concrete-mixer truck had trouble getting close enough to the hole to deposit its load. I was entertained by Tosh who happened to be home that day to watch the concrete pour. He tried to usurp the project manager's role and guide the driver past the house with a series of semaphore-like hand signals, which ensured the truck hit the side fence. The eyes of all the contractors present rolled as he shouted, "Who's going to pay for that?" The answer was obvious but Tosh was keen to dispute it. The manager, who no doubt had endured plenty of interfering clients in the course of his career, merely shrugged and instructed the driver to desist and depart, which would have left Tosh with a massive bill for a gaping hole in his back yard, along with a damaged fence and a tonne or more of unused concrete. It was a bluff that led to a capitulation and a begrudging apology. Then Tosh was politely asked to vacate the site so the pour could proceed without further interruption.

Most days, however, were boring. I spent a lot of my time reading books that Damien had recommended while we were still friends. These all seemed to have drug themes, by authors like Aldous Huxley and William Burroughs and Jack Kerouac. I read *On the Road* because Damien had insisted it showed us the way we should all live, but for me it was an unintended cautionary tale.

Once the pool was completed, the fence mended, and Tosh had celebrated with a party, which I avoided, locking the door to my room and watching *War and Peace* on video, I started to swim laps each morning. I had the pool to myself. Tosh had left for work, my mother had gone off with her personal trainer, while Pam remained inside, deeply involved in the application of cosmetics to her person, before she too headed for work. The water was a sanctuary. I had long lost my aversion to swimming once I discovered how solitary it was. With my head down I could almost believe the rest of the world with all its horrors and ugliness no longer existed. And that was a relief. My mental state was fragile. The psychotic attack had frightened me. I didn't want it to happen again. Whether it had been triggered by cannabis or my inability to cope with the slaughter of chickens or some other horror I didn't know, so it seemed a good idea to avoid everything that stressed me and also the substances I had used to deal with it. The pool was blue and empty and silent.

My mother was solicitous. She would sometimes join me on a banana lounge by the pool or bring a cup of tea to my room and ask me how I was doing.

"I've had enough, Mum. I don't want to go on. I don't think I can leave the house but I don't want to stay here with Tosher any longer. He loathes me, I loathe him."

"He doesn't loathe you. He doesn't even hate you, love. You've just got to learn not to push his buttons." She sighed. "I learned that a long time ago. I know you might find this hard to believe, but he's a lovely bloke, really. You're the only one that stirs him up. You bring out the worst in him. I'm not trying to blame you. It's just a clash of personalities."

"I've seen him hit you."

"Not often, Al."

"So, you're okay with that, are you?" I said in an incredulous tone.

"It only happens when I provoke him. I've learned to be careful. And smart. My girlfriends are the same. Their husbands are no different. It's just blokes, isn't it? It's in your nature. But most of the time Tosh and I get on like a house on fire."

"You know what I think? He's bullied you all your married life, and you've put up with it. But I can't. Not anymore."

Sitting on the side of my bed, she leant forward and gave me a brief hug, an awkward moment because we hadn't touched much since I became a teenager. "Can I tell you a secret, Al?" she said after some hesitation. "I shouldn't be saying this, but I don't really want you to become like him."

Her revelation stunned me, overwhelmed me. I couldn't stop the tears.

"Just get better, love." She smiled and left me alone.

It took me months before I found the courage to go out, at first on short excursions, down to the shops or for a walk beside the creek, or to the local library to borrow more books, but eventually I went further afield. I took the train to Geelong one day when the weather was pleasant and had a swim at Eastern Beach inside its famous sea baths. I started to visit the NGV, especially the Ian Potter Gallery, on a regular basis, studying its collections systematically. My intention was to build enough confidence to face the world again, not to be intimidated by its horrors, and to leave Tosh's place for good, to have nothing more to do with him. At least, of late, I hadn't seen much of him. He was working out ways to streamline his business, attending business seminars and conferences, seeking the miracle money-making formula. His absence helped my recovery.

One late autumn day, after viewing an exhibition of Pop Art, I wandered aimlessly around Southbank by the Yarra River, relieved the westerly blasts of wind had kept the tourist hordes away. I was reflecting on the exhibition, looking at the billboards I could see on buildings on the other side of the river, wondering what Warhol and Lichtenstein would have made of Melbourne, until I reached the casino at the far end of the promenade and headed inside out of the cold. Twice I had played blackjack there with Damien and Jonathan, who had devised what they thought was a winning system, which we employed without success. We were never asked to produce any proof of age, but this time a security guard accosted me. I presented ID, the fake kind most teenagers acquire, and was allowed to enter. I wanted a stiff drink rather than a hand of blackjack, and so I made my way to one of the luxury bars, pushing my luck with the dress code. But I was tolerated by the bar staff because business was relatively slow. I sat in a quiet corner drinking whiskey for a while, thinking I could do what the Pop Artists had done: rip off the commercial images around me and call it art. I had an eye for the crass and vulgar. I lived with it after all.

I was starting to feel tipsy when I set eyes on something that sobered me immediately. Tosh. He entered with a woman at his side. He was supposed to be in Sydney on a business trip, or at least that was what he had told Mum. He spoke to the woman, blissfully unaware of me, pointed her towards a sofa and went to the bar to order drinks. When he returned with the drinks and sat next to her, she leant towards him and rested her head upon his shoulder. His free hand rested on her thigh.

They drank and chatted for a while, until Tosh stood again to get more drinks. As he adjusted his trousers he looked around and noticed me. I was barely fifteen metres away. He grasped the backrest of a nearby chair to steady himself, his neck extended, the colour across his contorted face rising like mercury on a summer's day. He glanced at his companion who was unaware of me. Instead of heading for the bar he strode my way.

"What the hell are you doing here?" he hissed. "Have you been spying on me?"

I avoided answering by raising the whiskey in a mock toast.

"What's going on, you little sneak?"

I lowered the tumbler. "It's a very, very unpleasant coincidence," I said, my voice rising indignantly. "Go back to your—your girlfriend. Leave me alone."

"Look, it's not what it seems." His panicked eyes shifted from me to her momentarily.

She had turned to see what Tosh was up to and was staring at us, frowning. He gave her a gesture that probably meant he would explain everything. He repeated his claim in a hushed, dulcet tone, which culminated in a nervous chuckle.

"What is it then?"

"What are you doing in here? You're not even old enough."

"So, this is your Sydney business jaunt, is it?"

"Last minute change of venue, that's all."

"Change of city, too, apparently."

He sniffed back his nerves, came closer, and gripped my shoulder. "Don't get smart with me, boy. What would you know?"

He squeezed hard until I felt a sharp pain.

"Just leave me alone," I whined, my body beginning to shudder. "I don't care what you do."

He released me and looked towards the bar staff to see if they had noticed. I put the tumbler down and covered my face with both hands to conceal my emotions.

"What's the matter?" he said nervously. "You're not going to have another one of them fits, are you?"

"Does Mum know about her?"

"What? No, no." I noticed fear in his eyes. "This is business. Don't worry about her." His thumb pointed towards the woman. "She's just a business associate, that's all."

"What I saw looked more like pleasure than business."

"She was just having a joke. She's the over-friendly type. You know there's women like that."

"I might be crazy but I'm not stupid."

He dropped onto the chair next to mine, closed his eyes, and inhaled profoundly, like a yogi. "Okay, listen, Alan, listen. I want you to understand something. You're almost a man and you'll understand this as that bum fluff on your chin thickens up. I'm not getting any younger. And sometimes you've got to prove to yourself you've still got it, know what I mean?" He looked across at the woman who was still watching us. He gestured to her again. "For God's sake, Al, don't tell your mother, all right? It'd destroy her. I love her, you know that, don't you?"

"What about Mum?"

"I meant Mum, dickhead."

"You've got a funny way of showing it."

"This has got nothing to do with her."

"Go away," I pleaded. "I couldn't care less what you do. If Mum's been stupid enough to stay with you so long, that's her problem."

"Not a word then, please, Al," he implored.

Stunned, I watched him collect the woman and leave the bar; it was the first time he had begged me for anything.

14

I was no longer working at the chicken joint, but my mother gave me money, which kept me in cigarettes and not much else. She suggested that I should think about getting a driver's licence, merely because it was the normal thing for boys my age to do. I could apply for my learner's permit. She would pay for the lessons.

At first I declined. It seemed pointless. All the traffic was like madness to me. I felt too frail to face its aggression. But eventually I realised it might be a sensible step towards independence. The more I thought about it, the more enthusiastic I became. I could get a car. I could drive away. On the road. *On the road!*

When Mum raised it with Tosh, he had reservations. He questioned the wisdom of letting someone like me loose on the road.

Noticing my dejection, she responded, "He needs to be able to do something ordinary, like other young men. It can't do him any harm."

"It's not him I'm worried about."

Without going into any detail I reminded him of our chance meeting a few months earlier, and he changed his mind. "I'll give you lessons," he announced. "Why fork out money to some hopeless instructor when you've got me?"

When I demurred, he shrugged and acquiesced. It was a strange sensation, having a hold over him. It unsettled me. It didn't seem right. I changed my mind. "Okay," I said. "You can teach me."

"Let's go then. We might as well get started." He must have been afraid of my volatility. "We'll use your mother's car."

To my surprise he was patient with me. I made mistakes. He rarely raised his voice, just calmly pointed out the error and instructed how to correct it. He advised me not to lean over the steering wheel, unaware I was copying his driving technique. There were moments when I almost crashed and he showed signs of nervousness, which of course was contagious, but the only time he shouted was when a woman, with two small children in tow and pushing a pram, stepped onto a zebra crossing as I approached.

"Watch out!" he shouted, lunging at the steering wheel, causing us to swerve away. "You're supposed to give way!"

Despite the near miss, he had the temerity to ogle the young mother. After I resumed control of the car, he swivelled around to look through the rear window. "That would've been a waste of a good pair of legs," he mused, and when he realised I had heard, he added, "You know what? Your mother used to have legs like that."

"Let me concentrate."

He turned back to the road ahead of us. "She's let herself go," he grumbled. "That's what women do once they've hooked their bloke."

His lips flapped in a discontented expulsion of air.

I slammed on the brakes so hard his hands hit the dashboard in alarm.

"Shut up about Mum!" I yelled. "You show her a bit of respect or I'll tell her about that other woman."

He stared at me, wedged between impulse and prudence.

"Okay," he eventually muttered.

His acquiescence baffled me until I figured he probably feared the financial impact a divorce would have on his business.

Over the weeks my driving technique improved and he felt less need to comment. He just sat in the car while I accrued the necessary hours of instruction. While I drove through the suburbs he couldn't help looking at women in other cars or in the street, unaware of the desirous groans he sometimes emitted. When I drove along the freeway he often used the opportunity to catch up on some sleep.

I proved to be capable enough for Tosh to relax in the passenger seat, which is why I refused to accept any responsibility for the stroke he suffered towards the completion of my hours.

I was driving along a major thoroughfare when he groaned. I assumed he had spotted another attractive female. His body convulsed which I thought was a bit excessive, a bit too crass, even by his standards. I glanced his way and noticed something was awry. The jellyfish look was starker than usual and there was foam bubbling from one corner of his mouth, which seemed to be dragged down by an invisible hook. His eyes were focused on a spot high up on the windscreen as if he was staring at the dark angel.

"You all right?" I asked.

His garbled response convinced me something serious had happened. I pulled over near a pay phone and called for an ambulance.

One of the medics diagnosed a stroke once they had lifted him from the car onto a stretcher. "You've done the right thing, lad. You've probably saved his life."

With ambivalent emotions, I returned to the car, removed the L-plates, and drove home alone.

15

When my mother returned from the hospital with the news that Tosh would survive but have to spend months in rehab, she could barely conceal her relief behind a furrowed brow. His absence would change her life. During his recovery she was able to conduct her affairs without concerning herself with his reaction, a taste of freedom she hadn't experienced since her wedding day. She wore clothes I had never seen her in before and applied a different, sassier makeup, although never when she went to visit him, which only happened three times a week and always in daylight. She went out more often in the evenings, sometimes returning home well after midnight. I heard her singing and discovered she had her own taste in music. The only Rolling Stones song I heard her sing was *Get Off My Cloud* which I suspect she dedicated to Tosher. She preferred the music of Carly Simon, Carole King, James Taylor. She didn't bother me, although one day after a hospital visit she asked me to join her in the living room. "Your dad was asking after you today," she said, pouring coffee from a percolator, a recent addition to her kitchen. "He's upset you haven't been to see him yet."

I shrugged. "He never came to see me when I was in hospital. I'm returning the favour."

"I wish you wouldn't say things like that, Alan." She handed me a coffee in a tiny cup. "He does love you, you know, still, despite the trouble and worries you've caused him. He's had no luck at all. Neither you or Pam has shown any interest in the family business. You know it's under a lot of pressure, don't you? And now this stroke. Those managers are doing their best but they're no Ray McIntosh, are they?

What a blow this is for a man like him. He's never going to be the same, you know that, don't you?" An ambiguous noise tumbled from her.

We had become so estranged, she was unaware of what I knew or didn't know. I sipped the coffee, enjoying its sweet viscosity, making a loud appreciative sound with my lips. "That's good news for both of us."

"Oh, don't be so damn sarcastic, Al. You're always negative these days. I feel sorry for you, I really do." She looked away, blinking, on the verge of tears. "Heaven knows we've tried to give you the best of everything. That's partly the reason the business is in so much trouble. And what thanks do we get?" Her aggrieved gaze settled on me. "Have you ever thanked your father for what he's done for you? I think now would be a good time to do that, don't you?"

"Well, thanks, Dad, for the broken arm and broken nose, the punches, the loose teeth." I muttered. "I appreciate them and have learnt my lesson. Now I'm ready to become a junior partner in this wonderful business you've established, the profitable disposal of murdered corpses, with the intention of taking it over when you retire, and I'll look after you in your old age, changing your incontinence pads and wiping your cacky arse and wheeling you around while you dribble everywhere, especially in the sight of young women. We'll go feed the ducks down the park."

I was ranting and didn't notice how upset my mother had become.

"You're really nasty, you know that?" she interjected, raising her voice so I noticed and stopped. "I'm losing what's left of any respect I have for you, Alan. Okay, he's done some bad things to you but that's no excuse for you to be a bastard!"

I was shocked by her swearing but I couldn't relent. "Not long ago you were saying nice things about me and you didn't want me to change. So all that was bullshit, was it?"

She shrugged.

"When did you ever have any respect for me?" I began to shout. "You've always sided with him."

"He's my husband." She sighed, full of regret it seemed to me.

"You've called me a coward often enough. Maybe I inherited that from you."

She looked away, her jaw locked.

"How far does your loyalty go, Mum?" I added with cruel intent. "Does it include fidelity? I mean, what do you do on these late night-outs you've been having?"

She stared at me in anger. "What are you insinuating? You've got a filthy mind, my boy. Aren't I entitled to a bit of R-and-R after all these years? Not that I hold it against Tosh, but I finally get the chance to go out with a few friends and have some fun, friends I haven't seen in ages. What's wrong with that? I'm sure he wouldn't mind. But you, you make it sound sordid, dirty. Well, I can tell you I've done nothing I'm ashamed of. Never have, never will."

"That'll be a relief to Tosher."

"What do you mean, Tosher? It's Tosh. Tosher sounds like that rude English word. I've heard you call him that before. I wish you'd stop it. Anyway, he needn't know I go out some nights. He's got enough to worry about."

"I thought you said it was all innocent fun you're having."

"Of course it is, but he's going to worry, isn't he?"

"Let him. It's justice." I refrained from mentioning his little secret, which allowed me to feel less cruel, but I reminded her he had slapped her around enough in the past for no reason. "Do you think Pam and I aren't aware of what he's done to you? He's a control freak, Mum, can't you see that?"

She didn't answer immediately but sat with her eyes cast towards the ceiling before she uttered something astonishing. "Not anymore."

The period Tosh was kept in a rehab hospital was a pleasant time for the rest of us. I was no longer working at the chicken outlet. Pam was dating a young financial advisor who had wandered into the store where she worked to tell her she was the most beautiful chick he had seen in all of Chadstone Shopping Centre, but he might as well have said the world. Mum kept up her late-night socialising and slept in each morning. I ran into her one night when I was on my way to the toilet. She had just arrived home and she smelt of booze, cigarettes and, I was fairly sure, sex. I gave her a knowing smile and she reciprocated with a weary, sated nod.

I hoped she was fucking someone else, so deep was my contempt for Tosh. But when I spoke to Pam about it, she was scandalised. "Mum wouldn't do that!"

"Why not? She's just been trying to keep up with him, I'd say. What do you think *he's* been up to all these years, all the late nights, all them business conferences? You think they were about roast chicken?"

"You've got a filthy mind, Alan."

"Funny, that's what Mum reckons." We were alone, sitting by our pool on banana lounges in our bathers. I kept glancing at her bare body and the flimsy material covering those parts of her I liked to look at, had seen often enough through the bathroom window. "You want to know why?"

She rolled her head in my direction and lowered her sunglasses as if to indicate she was listening.

"When I was about thirteen our wonderful father first showed me pornography. To make a man out me. He hated having a wimpy son. A couple of years later he even took me to a strip joint to watch a woman getting fucked on stage."

She raised her knees defensively. "I don't believe you," she declared, although her voice quavered with uncertainty. "Why are you saying these nasty things about him now? Mum first, now Dad."

I laughed. "You know your problem, Pam? You're a deep-down good person. You can't find fault in anybody—except me, perhaps. You know what that makes you? Naïve. If you go through life being naïve, one day you're going to get badly hurt."

It was a balmy day. I rested my head against the plastic straps of the banana lounge and allowed a faint smile to curl the corners of my mouth. I felt years older than her.

She sat up sideways and placed her feet on the ground. Her hands gripped the frame of her lounge. She regarded me for a moment. "You need to leave home, Alan."

"Oh, yeah? Don't think I haven't thought about it, but where am I going to go?"

She stood up, facing me, her crotch covered in flimsy floral material a little above my eye level. She remained still. It seemed provocative. Her pubic bulge made my heart beat a little faster.

"If you had any guts you'd go. You don't belong here."

Suddenly she slapped my dick, which was going hard inside my swimming shorts. I doubled up, stunned more than in pain, almost having the banana lounge fold in on me. "Jesus!" I cried.

"I'm your sister not some whore."

She removed her sunglasses and dived into the pool.

16

It took Tosh four months after he left rehab to recover enough to return to work. Even so, a pitiful aura emanated from him. He walked with a dramatic limp. His face had changed shape. One cheek drooped, creasing the skin, creating a pattern of tiny grooves and dragging an eyelid lower. He no longer looked fierce but pathetic. His body had lost all its muscle tone. His spine had buckled below the neck. His hair had thinned so much you could see his scalp. His fringe was a few misplaced strands. His body was beginning to resemble some sketches I had seen of a decrepit Don Quixote. All he needed was a horse and lance.

He still tried to give orders, but they reached me in a shriek and had lost all authority. Most days I ignored him. My eighteenth birthday came and went. My mother and sister wanted me to celebrate, but I objected vehemently. I had no friends to invite. Any party would just be them. Me and them. How unbearable that would have been! I would look like a pathetic loner. I didn't mind being a loner, just not a pathetic one. Turning eighteen I lost my dependency status. Or, to put a more positive spin on it, I gained my independence. The government considered me an adult. It started paying me a pension related to my mental illness. It wasn't much, wasn't enough to purchase dope on a regular basis, which is what I wanted to do. I hankered for the refuge of a fuzzy brain. When Tosh asked me to pay for board I refused. Since he hadn't recovered sufficiently to get behind the wheel, he tried to coax me into driving him to and from his chicken outlets with a bit more money but not enough for dope. I reminded him that my driving lessons had been delayed and

I was yet to get my licence. But he told me to put the L-plates back on. He would be in the passenger seat as my instructor. I suggested he might have another stroke, and when he dismissed this with an impatient gesture, I warned him my proximity to his chicken joints might cause further psychotic episodes, especially if I had to sit around half the day, waiting for him, since I couldn't drive anywhere else on my own, which convinced him to drop the idea. Mum couldn't drive him all the time. It ended up costing him a fortune in taxi fees.

I kept hocking various possessions I had accumulated over the years that no longer held my interest, toys my mother or Tosh had given me—a Meccano set, a collection of Matchbox cars, archery equipment, a paintball gun I never used, a skateboard, roller blades, a model train set—but it wasn't enough to keep me in dope. I knew a few people, acquaintances of Sky, who were using other drugs—speed, ecstasy, heroin—but I wasn't interested in any of these or them. I managed to get my hands on some seeds and began to grow my own marijuana behind a shed at the bottom of our garden where Tosh no longer went and my mother never ventured. I was careful to tend my plants after dark, not that they needed much attention; they grew like weeds.

The heads they produced were potent. I sold a few to cover costs but never succumbed to the temptation of going into business, despite how lucrative I could see it would be. The world of commerce was anathema to me. Besides, I didn't have the right temperament. Increasingly I found it difficult to talk to people. No longer could I initiate a conversation, much less sustain it. If someone greeted me and appeared intent on chatting, my response, if I managed to say anything at all, was usually sullen and monosyllabic, which discouraged further interaction. The person would nod and shrug and move on, uncomfortable with the encounter. But it was not what I wanted. I would dearly have cherished a friendship; I just didn't seem to have the capacity to foster one when the opportunity arose.

In the year following my psychotic episode I was desperately lonely. There were moments when I felt so low I wanted to kill myself. And I'm certain I would have, had I not met—I should say become reacquainted with—Tiffany Sutherland, Damien's old girlfriend, who had been kind to me the few times I had been in her company when she felt others like Jonathan and Damien were making fun of me, although I actually thought I was being admired.

I had taken a bus along the Great Ocean Road, intent on drowning myself in the very spot Tosh had terrorised me when I was a kid, in the surf near Apollo Bay, hoping the symbolism wouldn't be lost on him when my body was found washed up along the coast somewhere. There was other symbolism too. Apollo was the god of music and dance, truth and prophecy, healing and diseases, god of the sun, light, poetry and protection of the young.

I was near the beach, staring in disappointment at a tame sea, when Tiffany approached.

"Is that you, Alan?"

I turned, alarmed at hearing someone call my name.

"I thought so!"

When I set eyes on her, I looked around for Damien.

"I spotted you from up there." She pointed towards the buildings behind the foreshore. "God, dude, it seems like years since I last saw you. You've shaved your head. I hardly recognised you."

My hand went to my head. I liked to keep my head bald; it made people wary of me.

"What are you doing here?" she asked.

I looked towards the cafe strip.

"I'm not with Damien," she said, guessing my concern. "Dumped him."

I shrugged, discomfited, and said nothing.

"He was a bloody narcissist."

"I thought you two were made for each other," I muttered, sounding bitter, resentful.

"You mean I was a narcissist too?" She chuckled, came close and hugged me. "It's good to see you, dude. But you look so unhappy."

"It's just the cold," I lied.

If I was unhappy, she looked radiant, even in the gloom of winter. Dressed in old jeans, a puffer jacket and runners, her beauty unsullied by cosmetics, she was shedding her adolescence without resorting to artifice. I felt my chest constrict.

"I heard you've been down on your luck," she said, holding me at arm's length to observe me earnestly.

"That's the polite way of putting it."

She nodded earnestly, as if she understood. "Listen, why don't we go somewhere and have a coffee?"

Surprised that anyone at all had been talking about me lifted my spirits a tad. It was ridiculous, I know, but I was grateful. I hadn't disappeared entirely from the minds of my erstwhile friends. And as absurd as it sounds, my existence felt affirmed, if only tangentially. I agreed to a coffee.

Since I had my hands in the pockets of my leather jacket, she threaded her arm through mine companionably and chatted as we walked to the street above the beach, animated by our chance encounter a couple of years after we had last seen each other. She told me she had dropped out of uni and started to study film-making at the School of the Arts and had come down along the coast looking for a location for the project she had undertaken, a short movie about a shipwreck, based on an historical tragedy. I had avoided answering her question about my reason for being here but now she asked again. "I watched you for a little while as you were staring at the sea," she added, "and I wondered what you were thinking about."

"I just needed to get out of the city," I said. "It gets me down."

"Yeah, I know what you mean." There was an inflection of sympathy in her voice.

I appreciated it. When we were seated in a cafe, I studied her. Nothing got her down, I could tell. Her expression, her entire body exuded optimism, enthusiasm, joy.

"You looked like you were about to walk into the sea," she chided.

Her observation unsettled me. For a moment I felt paranoid, suspecting she had been sent to prevent me doing something stupid. By whom? Somebody. She noticed and realised she had come close to the truth. "Not a good idea," she cried. "You'd ruin a good leather jacket." Her head tilted and eyebrows rose to let me know she was attempting a joke.

So I made light of her insight. "I was thinking about swimming to Tassie—get away from it all."

"There's easier ways to get there."

"Not if you're trying to make the Guinness Book of Records there isn't. Fame is what we all seek."

"I didn't think you were into that sort of thing."

She leant back, drew her auburn hair from her face as if she wanted to make a ponytail.

"What're they doing these days?" I asked. "Damien, Jonathan, Patrick?"

She glanced at me sharply. "You haven't heard?"

She would have known they had distanced themselves from me. I shrugged and shook my head.

"Damien's doing his Masters, apparently."

She hesitated, looking around, pretending something had distracted her.

"And the others?"

"Jonathan's dead."

"What?"

"You really are out of touch, aren't you?"

I felt the muscles in my gut tighten. "What happened?"

Her jaw tightened for a moment. "Suicide."

I returned her gaze blankly but her revelation affected me badly. "You don't sound too upset," I said, observing her as she finished with her hair.

"Why should I be?"

"He was a friend, wasn't he? Or did that end too, when you dropped Damien?"

"He was an arsehole. He blamed me for his girlfriend, sweet Jodie, walking out on him. Couldn't face the truth."

"Which was?"

"He used to enjoy doing things to her that she didn't like, so I encouraged her to end the relationship. And you know what he did? He raped me for it. He called me an interfering bitch and he raped me."

"Fuck, Tiffany, that's not Jonathan. He'd never do that."

"Oh, I'm a liar, am I?"

"No, no, but—"

She wouldn't let me finish. "Ah, so, you're another who's one going to make excuses for him."

"That's not the Jonathan I knew."

"It never is, is it, with you guys."

"Did you go to the cops?

"Ha! A lot of good that would've done."

"What did you do? Surely—"

"When he got off me, I laughed at him. I said, 'No wonder Jodie left you.'" Tiffany wasn't looking at me. Her eyes were on the sea. "He started to cry and apologized, the bastard."

"Did you tell Damien?" I examined her profile wondering if she was exaggerating. "What did he say? Were you still going out with him when this happened?"

"Well, Damien—he was so understanding, wasn't he. You know what he did? He just shrugged and said, 'Jonathan's an idiot, don't worry about it.' And, you know what, they carried on with their friendship as if nothing had happened."

She turned her head and regarded me with a defiant expression, expecting me to defend them. I felt guilty by an association long ago abandoned. I squirmed. "I haven't seen either of them since I left the school. Why do you think he killed himself? Because he felt guilty about what he did to you, or what?"

"Ha!" She shuddered and raised her chin and said nothing for a moment. "He said—in a note—he said it was because Jodie wouldn't go back with him. After she dropped him he stalked her, confronted her in public, started fights with any guy she went out with, threw a rock through her bedroom window when he thought she was in there with someone.

And he'd raped her best friend. Do you think she was likely to go back with him? In the end she had to get an intervention order taken out against him. And so he goes and tops himself and blames her. Poor Jodie. It's affected her badly."

I could see the anger in her face. She glanced at me with a defiant smile. A waitress arrived. We ordered coffees.

"How did Damien take it?" I asked after the waitress moved off.

"Him? He blamed me. He said I was an interfering bitch. He said I encouraged Jodie to leave Jonathan, to hurt him. He said I was playing power games. Can you believe that? You guys—I tell you, you're as thick as thieves."

"What about Patrick?" I asked. "What did he think?"

"Don't know, didn't ask." She took several sachets of sugar from a bowl and spent some time designing patterns with them on the table top. "You know he's set up a computer business, don't you? He's making a fortune apparently."

"What?" I gaped. "What happened to the revolution?"

"I ran into him in South Yarra six months ago, and that's exactly what I asked him." Her laugh was silent. "He reckons capitalism's got to run its course before anything like that will happen. So he's helping it along. These days being a wealthy entrepreneur is the best thing you can do for the revolution, apparently, but don't ask me, politics was never my thing. I don't think he sees Damien much anymore. But I wouldn't know for sure. It's just what I hear."

We both looked towards the counter wanting our coffees to arrive. An awkward silence settled over us until, as if it were an urgent matter she had forgotten to raise, she suddenly asked, "How did your high schools exams go? Did you get into uni, Al?" Her eyebrows were raised, hopeful, for my sake. She reached over and squeezed my forearm, which was resting on the table.

I lowered my eyes, remembering how she used to encourage me to do well at school so we could keep our little coterie together. How I had wanted that! Now I realised my estrangement had little to do with it falling apart, which would have happened with or without me.

"No. No uni. These days I'm a psycho."

She chuckled, thinking I was joking.

"No shit," I went on. "Psychotic stuff. Voices in the head. That sort of fabulous company."

She nodded silently, her head forward in an attempt to conceal her surprise with an expression of concern.

Our coffees arrived and she made a point of chatting to the waitress about the surf being flat and the lull in tourists as if she were a local, gaining time to readjust her perception of me, the nutter. I added three sugars to my coffee and stirred solemnly.

"Where are you staying?" she asked me, once the waitress had retreated.

"Nowhere."

"This's just a day trip then, is it?"

I shrugged and looked away, unwilling to voice what she had probably guessed already—I was on a one-way ticket.

"How would you like to come and meet my crew? We're going further along the coast tomorrow, if you're interested. There's a really great little cove we want to check out. It could be the right place for the survivors of the shipwreck to come ashore. Are you still interested in the arts, mate? I'd love you to read my screenplay and then I can pick your brains about any improvements you think could be made."

She put the coffee to her lips and her eyes were gleaming.

Her generosity almost had me crying. "Okay. Why not? Thanks."

The smile she offered was perfect—spontaneous and genuine. "Here," she said, pulling a manuscript from her shoulder bag. "Have a squiz. See what you think."

A serious expression crossed her face and she stared at me for a moment. "I can tell you're wondering why I'm bothering to talk to you."

I shrugged and began to feel uneasy.

"Well, I always knew you were different. You're sweet. Damien told me you had a brutal father. A lot of guys would've ended up violent bastards themselves. But I'm pretty sure not you. You're still an innocent. That's the word to describe you."

I shamed myself by bursting into tears. Tiffany was shocked.

"Sorry, sorry," I blubbed. "I'm in a bad place at the moment."

"Hey, mate," she said, touching my arm. "You're going to be all right."

"I'm not used to kindness."

Her phone rang. It startled me. It was early days for mobile phones. I didn't own one. She took it from her bag but hesitated, looking at me as if she needed my permission to answer.

"It's fine. I'm okay."

"Scusi," she said and slipped away to take the call.

I pulled myself together and read through the script. It was only about twenty pages with minimum dialogue, a short film, as she had said, a student film, about a group of Scots whose sailing ship is wrecked in a storm in the early nineteenth century. All but two young women drown. They are rescued by some local Aborigines who offer them food and shelter and treat their injuries. The women are taken to a hill one day, once they had recovered, and they survey the land before them. One of them comments that it would make great farmland. There is a strange noise over the hill behind them and they are led by their Aboriginal guide to investigate. There's a modern highway and a group of bikies. The women break away from their guide and run towards the bikies, yelling for help. The bikies threaten the guide, who looks utterly bewildered. The women jump onto pillion seats and are taken away, leaving the guide alone on the hilltop shaking his head and saying in an Aboriginal language, "What a bunch of savages!" (subtitled).

Tiffany saw I was grinning when she returned. "You like it?" Her voice was hopeful and slightly anxious.

"It's hilarious. I love that last scene."

"If it works out, I want to enter it in the Short Film Festival. You heard of that?"

"It'll win, for sure."

"Al, I haven't even made it yet!" She was so pleased with my response she came to my side of the table and gave me a hug and a kiss on the cheek. Its warmth pervaded my body like a drug. Another thing, she took a rustic woollen beanie from her bag and pulled it onto my head, down over my ears. "There," she said. "You look cute now."

"You might need it," I said, assuming it was hers.

"I just bought it for you, dude, at the shop next door. Please, keep it."

It took a tremendous effort not to burst into tears again.

When I stood, she grasped my arms and regarded me with an earnest expression. "Can I give you some advice, mate? Talk to your father. Stay calm. Be honest with him. If he listens, good. You might be able to resolve some of the issue between you. If he doesn't, too bad. But you'll be surprised at how liberating that will be. Take my word for it. I've had a similar experience."

I spent the next two days with her, meeting her crew, a diverse bunch of sociable and unsociable types, staying overnight on the verandah sleepout at the holiday cottage she had rented for a few days, accompanying them an hour further along the coast to the cove she had spoken about, where arguments ensued over the technical difficulties of staging a credible shipwreck on their meagre budget. It was my idea to change the first scene from an actual sinking of the schooner to a bit of debris and a few bodies washing ashore and then shots of an empty sea, which was applauded by all.

"I'll have to add your name to the credits," Tiffany said with a grin.

I shrugged but was secretly thrilled. It surprised me how thrilled I was. The crew did some filming and some sound and light tests, while I sat on the beach watching, my depression lifting like coastal mist with a weak sun breaking through, beginning to warm my psyche. Maybe Apollo was looking down on me, after all.

One of the crew came over and dropped onto the sand beside me, a short man with receding hair and a pencil moustache. "I don't have much to do here," he said. "I'm down as the editor. Most of my work will be back at college. But I wanted to come and see this place." He carried a laptop, which he opened to look at some of the trial rushes already downloaded and muttered something about the light being too bright for a shipwreck scene. "I can see a problem with sand getting into this," he added, referring to the computer. He watched the other film students still discussing logistics and camera angles further along the beach. "This is the life, isn't it? Wouldn't you like to do this for a living?"

He wasn't really after my thoughts about a career in movies. Rather, he was wistfully thinking of his own future. But he turned to me and said, "You're a natural, you know that? Your idea for the start of this scene was straight out of Ingmar Bergman's handbook, which is great because the finale, the scene with the bikies, as you probably figured, references Mad Max. And now, with your contribution, it's become a tribute to the entire spectrum of movie making. You've managed to give it an overarching context. Some achievement, man."

He offered to high-five me, and my tardiness with the uptake he mistook for modesty, when in reality I had no idea what he was talking about. Still, I was in a state of mind too fragile to disabuse him.

"You'll go places, for sure." He nodded earnestly as he watched the rest of the crew who were moving along the beach near the water's edge, gesticulating and huddling to discuss ideas. "Where'd you say you're studying film?"

"I'm not."

"Really?" He levered himself to his feet and brushed the sand from his jeans. "You should." He trotted away and joined the others.

I was delighted he thought I had achieved something brilliant even if I had only the vaguest idea what he was talking about. Being the object of admiration was an entirely new experience for me. I reclined and stared at the clouds drifting by, wallowing in the intoxicating sensation. I was someone impressive—at least to one other person. It had been a long time coming.

17

The next day I went back to Melbourne with Tiffany in one of the crew's cars and shifted almost immediately into the house she shared with a few of the other students. It was a grand old double-storey terrace not unlike the one Damien's parents owned but in a less salubrious neighbourhood. It must have had four or five bedrooms, plus a tiny windowless space that used to be a cloakroom, converted to a *boudoir*, as the tenants facetiously called it, with the simple addition of a mattress on the floor and a cheap chest of drawers. I was offered the boudoir, vacated a week earlier by a fellow student film maker who had dropped out of the course and gone home. It was dingy and airless but infinitely preferable to the alternative.

A week later, in the middle of the day when I knew Tosh would be at one of his franchises, I went to collect the rest of my clothes, my laptop and my dope paraphernalia, and to say goodbye to Cassius, who was miraculously still alive, had reached an ancient doggie age, walked with stiff legs but still wagged his tail each time he saw me. I would miss him more than anyone else in the house. I wasn't yet ready to take up Tiffany's suggestion to talk calmly to Tosh about how he had treated me all my life, despite my resolve to do so.

My mother arrived home as I was walking out the door with a couple of large bin liners full of my possessions. "Where have you been?" she demanded. "What are you doing?"

"I'm shifting out of this crap place. This isn't a home, not mine anyway. Never has been."

She slapped my face, the first time in her life she had hit me. It astonished both of us. She looked around to see if anyone had witnessed it. Relieved we were alone, she added, "After all we've done for you this is how you treat us."

"You're turning out just like him," I said without much conviction.

"We've been worried sick, wondering where you've been—whether you're still alive or not."

"Well, here I am. Never felt better." I rubbed my stinging cheek and affected a smile to show I meant it.

"I don't suppose you care your father's back in hospital."

"Another stroke?"

"Don't sound so happy about it, Alan. It was his heart this time. He's been so worried about you."

"Oh, so, it's my fault again."

"You disappearing didn't help."

"He was so worried he came looking for me, did he? I suppose he went to the cops to report me missing? Organised a search party?"

"He didn't want to trouble the police again."

"That was considerate of him."

"You haven't even asked how he is." She sounded genuinely baffled.

"Not my most pressing concern."

"He's your father!"

"Is he? I have my doubts."

"What are you insinuating?"

My smile must have looked supercilious as I elaborated. She slapped my face again, as if she was beginning to enjoy the tactic. I winced but didn't whimper.

"You don't appreciate me at all, do you?" she said. "Do you think my life's been easier than yours?"

I picked up my luggage. "I'm sorry, Mum. You've been good to me, but I've got to get on with my own life. I can't do it here."

18

One thing led to another. I played a minor part in Tiffany's movie, as one of the dead bodies washed up on the shore, and then on a hired motorcycle as one of the bikies, which was fun, although the film was never the success we all thought it would be. But at the short film festival I met Eileen Caitlin Quinn, a chain-smoking, stout-drinking, fusty, middle-aged screen writer. Tiffany had told her about my contribution to *Shipwreck*'s script and she cornered me in a beer garden at a pub close to the festival venue. "You want to be one of us, eh?" she said lighting up, since smoking was yet to be banned outdoors. "Well, let me give you some advice, young fellow."

The advice was that she, EC, as she insisted I call her, would take me under her wing and teach me everything she knew about writing for TV as well as the big screen. She earned a living writing for a soapie that was syndicated across Australia and abroad. I would be her protege. I would shift into her house in Caulfield and she would give me two hours of her day, five days a week, in tutelage, in return for sex whenever she needed it, although this wasn't spelt out at the beer garden meeting; I learnt about it soon after I became her lodger. The only other demand she made of me was to resist the lure of money. "Don't stoop to insincerity. Always write with conviction, even if you only write soapies, as I do these days."

My bedroom duties were the easiest part of the agreement, usually performed late at night after some fairly heavy drinking in front of the TV, watching videos of past episodes of the soapie she worked on. EC was nearly as old as my mother and a damn sight less attractive. I feared she would be repulsive in bed but I was mistaken. She was sensual, at times lascivious, never boring, never basic like Sky had been. No doubt she thought she was the lucky one but I soon realised fortune lay with me. Not only was I learning a lot about the amorous arts but my daytime lessons were equally illuminating. She taught me the importance of narrative tension, with all its rhythms, and the complexities of characterisation. She encouraged me to develop scenes for the soapie, first collaboratively and then reducing her contribution until I was writing entire episodes, which were submitted under her moniker without any of the production team recognising the authorial difference. I received a commission from her for all services rendered.

EC was pleased with my progress and privately proud of her mentorship. Within six months she introduced me to the team and persuaded its mercurial members to offer me a place at the table, which is how my career in TV production began, how the soapie became more edgy and dark, moving into thriller territory, how its popularity soared.

Neither of us, as far as I know, mentioned our nocturnal routine to anyone else. It was our secret. In fact we never discussed it at all, even when we were alone together. When I started dating other, younger women, EC was unperturbed. It actually seemed to her like a clever decoy after some of her friends started speculating. She would ask me to show up with my latest girlfriend and went out of her way to endear herself, acting maternally towards me, whereby any inkling of our scandalous liaison fizzled.

Unlike me, EC was a convivial creature. There was nothing she enjoyed more, outside our bedroom romps, than to head for a pub, preferably one with live music, preferably of the Celtic variety, for she was, in her own words, a sentimentalist—Irish through and through. I had no interest in this ancestral stuff, although everyone I knew seemed to want to belong somewhere, to be part of something greater than themselves, as if this would give their lives some meaning and help overcome the horror of an ephemeral existence. Nevertheless, it was a pleasure to hear her hold court once she had downed a few pots of the dark libation that anyone of Celtic origin approached with religious solemnity.

Despite her own predilection for substance abuse, she wouldn't countenance me smoking dope in her house. "If you want to do that, you'll have to leave," she insisted when she first encountered me stoned in her living room, which was more effective in breaking my dependency than any detox treatment.

One day the production of our soapie took us to the Chadstone Shopping complex where my sister still worked, in the donut store whose franchise Tosh had once tried to acquire. I called on her, just to inform her how well I was doing since I left home. I wanted her to know I had become quite a celebrity within the industry, which was neither here nor there to me, except in the sense that it was totally beyond any influence or input from Tosh. She took a break, and we went and had a coffee.

Pam wasn't entirely pleased to see me. She talked for a while about how upset she and our mother had been with my departure. She accused me of being as hurtful as Tosh. And when I objected to the comparison, she said, "He's changing, you know. He's found Jesus."

I burst into laughter. "That's preposterous."

She disagreed by shrugging. "After his heart attack, one of his managers—you know Matt?—he took to visiting Dad in hospital, spent a lot of time with him, and apparently raised enough capital to save the franchises, which kept Dad out of the bankruptcy courts."

"Matt the proselytiser?"

"The what?"

"Matt the missionary."

"Whatever. The bloke you worked for."

"Yeah, I remember him. I know his church quite well. I was in its clinic, remember?"

She nodded. "Mum reckons he got the money through his church. I don't know what the arrangement was. I think Dad has to pay it all back. But Matt insisted it was because Jesus loved Ray McIntosh, you know, personal-like, and Dad went along with it. He started going to church every Sunday."

I stared into my coffee trying to picture it: Tosh in a suit, his shoes polished, his logoed cap abandoned, trying to look humble.

"He drags Mum along, too. And I've been a few times just to please him. Funny to see him waving his hands around in the air and singing them hymns about how Jesus loves him. I don't know whether I believe but it's fun. Everyone there's so nice to us. And Dad, he's stopped swearing and things. He's forgiven you, you know. You should come and see him. Make up."

"He's forgiven me? Well, that's fucking generous of him. After all the wrong I've done him."

"Yeah, I think so."

"You think so? You think so!"

"Shhh! Keep your voice down." She looked around, embarrassed.

"Fuck, Pam, it's time *you* shifted out of home," I went on, but more subdued. "Get a life of your own. Whatever happened to that art teacher you had a crush on?"

"What? I don't know."

"Maybe you should've kept in touch with her, followed your heart."

"I don't know what you're suggesting. That's disgusting. What are you becoming, Al?"

"Despite Tosh's best attempts, a decent person, I hope."

"That's not what I've heard."

"What have you heard?"

"You're living with an older woman, much older."

I tried my best to hide my surprise. "I share a house with one, if that's what you mean."

"Are you sure it's not her bed you're sharing?"

"Where did you hear this?"

"It's around, Al, you can't deny it. You should be ashamed of yourself."

I jutted my chin forward. "Oh, yeah?"

"Dad knows. You didn't ask how he was, by the way."

"See you, Pam. Thanks for asking me about my job."

Her head jerked back, a little ashamed. "I was going to."

I tossed some money on the table for our coffees and went back to the crew.

Of course, I knew what she was talking about. EC and I were involved in what I considered a minor scandal. It happened at the national TV awards night. Our popular soapie was up for several awards. The lead male was Todd Buckley, who was also making a name for himself as a pop star, appearing on various morning shows, on social networks, in video clips, and the rest. He had been nominated for the best actor award. A recent addition to our cast, Coco Cuthbertson, was on the best new face or some such award. My name appeared on the best screenplay list, while EC was up for a lifetime achievement award. EC had arranged for me to arrive with Coco, while she coupled up with one of our ageing producers. Buckley strutted the red carpet with his publicity-savvy wife, received most of the media attention, and was last to arrive at our table. I noticed him wink at Coco. I was seated on one side of her; EC on the other. I believe EC noticed too. She looked past Coco and raised an eyebrow, as if to suggest to me a direction our soapie could take. I received my award and said little more than thank you to the audience. Buckley managed to irritate most of our production team with a pithy oration on his extraordinary talent. EC, who was inebriated by the time she was called to the stage, gave a long-winded speech on the parlous state of TV production and the arts in general thanks to the deliberate budgetary neglect of successive governments, before a perfunctory statement of gratitude. She stumbled descending the stairs on her return to our table to general amusement, saved only by an attentive convention-centre staff member.

The drama really began when Buckley winked at Coca again, and she complained quietly to EC that he had sexually assaulted her in her dressing room earlier in the day. I heard EC mutter, "I've heard he's a sleaze." Then, slurring, she called across the table, "Hey, Buckley, does your pretty young wife know you interfere with other women? What's your name, sweetheart? Do you know you're married to a sexual predator?"

Buckley was stunned. "What are you talking about? You're drunk." He thrust his head forward across the table. "Be careful of what you accuse me."

EC hadn't lost her wits to the booze completely. She didn't name Coca, who wasn't the first female on the set of our soapie to utter similar accusations. "Talk to any of our female colleagues," she retorted. "They all tell the same story about you."

"All except you, I suppose, you sad geriatric sop. The only bloke who'd bed you is that pathetic jerk there." He pointed a finger quivering with indignation at me.

"You arsehole!" She was getting to her feet, full of righteous fury. "You'd be nothing without us. We write what you make your money and fame from. We made you! Don't you ever forget that, you twerp!"

Now the revellers on the tables around us were watching, gripped by a real drama and not some goggle-box nonsense.

EC rounded the table unsteadily until she was behind him. Buckley didn't deign to turn towards her. He didn't notice that somewhere on her journey she had picked up a jug of water, until she emptied it over his head.

He roared. Cameras were flashing. Shouts of outrage and amusement were all around. I swear my heart jolted. I jumped out of my seat to reach EC before others did, but I wasn't quick enough to prevent Buckley's affray. He slapped her on the neck which sent her tumbling sideways. She landed on a hapless guest, and both crashed to the floor. The cameras all around were rewarding their investors. I helped EC to her feet and led her, half carried her, out of the building. I heard Buckley shout, "You two are a disgrace." He avoided expletives, mindful of the media coverage.

EC was charged with assault. Buckley escaped any such ignominy, being one of the nation's favourite personalities. The whole tawdry affair was in the papers and on TV. Much was made of EC having a lover half her age. Tosher could hardly have failed to hear about it.

One day, after I thought the angles of EC's public shaming had been exhausted, I was approached by a tabloid journalist who demanded I come clean about my living arrangements. I told her to piss off, calling her a gutter rat—a big mistake, offending a tabloid bloodsucker, because it shifted her focus from public scandal to personal vendetta. What outraged me the most, though, wasn't the headline—HE'S YOUNG ENOUGH TO BE HER SON—or the grainy paparazzi photo of me consoling EC after we left the awards event, taken from an adjacent park and a reminder to keep the emotions private—although that was egregious enough. No, it was the photo of me in a drug-addled state under a bridge when I was a teenager. There was only one source for that.

The entire article was a comprehensive attempt to besmirch EC through her amorous predilections and her choice of lover. There were quotes from my ex-girlfriends, quotes from disaffected colleagues whose toes I had apparently stood on (although I always tried to work collegiately), even a quote from EC denying any romantic attachment to me. The journalist had gone to great lengths to chase down students I went to school with, including Damien, who said I was "a lost soul", and Sky—how they located her, I have no idea—who described me as "a wild beast" and "Patrick Ashcroft on steroids". The only ones who spoke in my favour were Tiffany and other members of her original crew. Tiffany described me as "misunderstood, very creative, kind-hearted", but her opinion was lost under the deluge of criticism. Most of the article relied upon an extensive interview with my father, just out of hospital and pictured in his dressing gown and pyjamas, who, according to the journalist, denounced me as a major contributor to his declining health, a life-long recalcitrant, an uncontrollable son, a teen-age drug addict, and a mentally unstable sociopath, whose attitude had encouraged a former schoolmate to suicide. This was all in the name of sanitising our leading man's role in the scandal.

When I went to speak to Tosher about it, I tried to keep Tiffany's advice in mind. Stay calm. Talk rationally about the impact he had had on my life. Be dignified.

"Why the fuck did you say I had something to do with Jonathan killing himself?" I screamed, waving my copy of the tabloid newspaper in front of him.

"Thanks for asking how I'm doing," he said lamely. "How long's it been since you come to see me?"

"Answer the fucking question!"

"I never said that. I didn't even know about it," he protested. "I mentioned your friends' names but she must've found out somewhere else about him topping himself and your friendship going sour, and she's gone and put two and two together."

I tried to calm down. "Have you any idea how this makes EC look?"

"Who?"

"My lover, you dick."

"Oh, so you care what people think, do you? That's new."

"I couldn't care less about myself. But EC!"

Pam had said he had changed now he had found Jesus, but except for the physical deterioration due to his illnesses he seemed no different. He was reclining on a banana lounge by his pool in skimpy nylon bathers, smoking a cigarette and reading the sports pages of the tabloid that had published the article about me. My mother wasn't at home. She interstate visiting a relative, and Pam was at work, but there was another woman on the other side of the pool in the shade of a sun umbrella.

"Who's she?"

"Just a neighbour taking advantage of my pool and my hospitality. It's a sunny day."

I was too upset about his contribution to the defamatory article to ask her name. I ignored her. I slapped my copy with the back of my hand. "How much did they pay you?"

He looked at me through his sunglasses for a moment. "Just like you to think the worst of me."

"How much?" I muttered, tossing the paper away, its loose pages fluttering onto the surface of the pool.

"I figured you owed me."

"Jesus Christ!"

"I wish you wouldn't use the Lord's name in vain, Alan."

"How much?"

"I can't say. Business confidentiality and all that. But not enough to make up for all the money I've spent on you over the years."

"This is the pits. It's unforgivable, Dad. And, you know something, I wouldn't have expected anything different from you."

I saw some of the old anger stirring in his eyes and the way his shoulders twitched. "I wasn't going to worry you with this, but I won't have you thinking I'm the bastard here. You know my health's suffering. And, you know what? Your mother, she blames you, all the grief you've given me over the years. There's been times when I've had to neglect my business to deal with you, which pushed my franchises to the brink. And this latest episode, with my heart, it's put me out of operation for who knows how long. I've had a lot of trouble keeping solvent, so when that reporter came round asking for some background on you, I could've just told her and would've, but I saw an opportunity. What difference did it make, me getting a bit out of it, to help the business? It wasn't much. You're not that famous. I only told the truth. God's my witness."

"The only witness we've got is over there." I pointed at the woman. "Otherwise I'd have tossed you in the bloody pool by now."

He looked towards his guest, a wistful expression troubling his crooked lips.

"My guess is she's someone else you're screwing or hoping to," I added. "And in your state—what a farce that would be."

"Keep your voice down."

Suddenly, I felt deflated, disgusted, loathing my belligerence. "I'm not like you," I muttered to myself. "I don't want to be like you."

I walked away.

"I'm proud you've turned your life around," he called in a voice high-pitched and squeaky, probably due to his earlier stroke. "Winning prizes. You've really surprised us, Al. You've made a success of yourself. That's all I ever wanted. I told the reporter that too but she didn't put it in."

"Success is the last thing I care about," I said, loud enough for him to hear, without looking back.

19

EC took the scandal surrounding the article worse than I did. It portrayed her as a predatory old floozie. She took to the stout heavily. Late one evening, a couple of months after its publication, she was on her way home from the pub when she stumbled from a tram into the path of a car that failed to give way. It was Saint Patrick's Day, if I remember rightly.

I was distraught, incapable of organising her funeral. But EC had loyal friends, and they arranged it. An old thespian who had once been her lover, well before I came on the scene, gave the eulogy, which mercifully downplayed my role in her life, highlighted his own. I sat alone and stifled my grief.

The wake was a drunken celebratory affair which would have pleased EC. I left before it became too maudlin, went to her house and onto our unmade bed. I wept into her pillow.

20

Tiffany Sutherland came to my aid once more. She understood my vulnerability, helped me through my grief, made sure I didn't relapse into any of my addictions, other than whiskey, perhaps, and she helped me find another place to live, since I didn't feel I could survive alone in EC's house.

We were lovers for a while but I realised soon enough she was only trying to console me. It ended at the airport. She was shifting to Los Angeles to further her career. We exchanged best wishes.

A few months later and still grieving EC, my mother rang. "It's your dad."

"What about him?"

"They've found cancer."

"Who has?"

"Them doctors did all these tests on Tosh after his heart attack. Lung cancer, Al."

"A triple whammy. The medical hat trick," I chuckled softly. "First a stroke, then heart attack. Now this."

"It's already spread. He hasn't got long to go. A couple of months the doctors reckon, that's all."

She began to cry.

"The chooks will be pleased."

"What?"

"The chooks. His franchises, remember?"

"Nobody's going to stop eating chicken because your father can't run the business anymore." She spat her words like poison. "Someone else is taking it over."

"I can't guess who." Irony was now my forte. "That's a pity. Slaughtering animals for food should be banned."

"Is that all you can think of?" Indignant and tearful, she waited vainly for my apology. "You remember Matt, the manager where you worked until—."

"Until my psycho episode, yeah, I remember."

"Tosh owes him some money. A lot of money, actually. Matt's been kind enough to oversee the business. It spares us a lot of financial complications. But I want you to come home. I can't cope on my own."

"Tosh's at home, is he?"

"He's in hospital but Pam and I are visiting him every day. Neither of us is coping very well, Al. We need a bit of moral support. Your father's dying. Doesn't that mean anything to you?"

"It means a lot."

"Well, come home, just until he goes, or a bit longer if you want," she said, struggling to speak. "Please. Whatever you think, he is your father and he's not going to last much longer."

I was silent, unwilling to agree.

"He's always wanted the best for you," she said. "And he only ever wanted to get the best out of you. You were his only son."

"Funny way of showing it. He suffocated me."

"Do you think you would've got to where you are today without him, you winning prizes and getting your photo in all them magazines, getting on the tellie? Please, Al, come and stay until he passes. If not for him, for me. For my sake."

I paced the room. The Tosher's imminent demise animated me. At last I would be free of him. And my mother, despite all her faults and weaknesses, didn't deserve my hostility.

"You know," she added, "Tosh was so delighted he had a son he used to throw you way up in the air."

21

I went back to be with my mother until Tosh died.

Predictably, the evangelical chook outlet manager, the gormless Matt Harrison, started visiting her, all rectitude, to offer any help she needed, "to get you through these trying times that God's given you. He works in mysterious ways, Alice. It's a trial but I know you'll put your faith in the Lord, and you'll pull through."

She burst into tears and before a week was out, with him coming around each night, she wasn't just pulling through. She was pulling something else as well, I was sure.

But I couldn't have cared less. Good luck to her, I thought.

I wasn't keen to see Tosh but Pam insisted I participate in a roster, sharing time at his bedside. He was in a private ward with tubes and monitors attached to various limbs and chest. The cancer had affected his respiration. With a bit of effort he could still talk, although he sounded like one of those old vinyl records played at a higher speed. I took a book along and ignored him most of the time, grunting responses when he tried to ask me for something until he gave up. His illness worsened much faster than his doctor predicted. Within a couple of weeks he lost ten kilos, his skin was grey, his eyes were dull and sunken, his nose and mouth covered with an oxygen mask. I was surprised and a tad shamefaced about my rising spirits.

One night I was alone in the private ward with him. Mum had gone home, having spent the afternoon and evening at his side, waiting, hoping. It was my turn for the graveyard shift. The night nurse had checked on him and returned to her station, giving me a sympathetic look as she left. The only noises were distant sirens and the regular ping from his monitors. I was reading the book at his bedside when he began to speak. I thought he asked me to smother him.

Was it just my mind playing tricks? "What?"

"You heard. Smother me."

My mind clunked like an old car's faulty gearbox. I sat upright in the visitor's chair, jarring my neck, lurching from an uneasy lethargy. In the cot beside me, he had removed his oxygen mask.

"I can't do that," I mumbled.

"Can't you just do what I ask for once in your bloody life?"

My heart raced. The possibility of it! "You know what would happen to me if I did, don't you?"

He coughed and wheezed and finally muttered, more to himself than to me: "You've been the greatest disappointment of my life, bar none."

Smother him. He had spent his whole life smothering me.

He took a rasping breath. "I won't ask again." He seemed to be losing his marbles. Did he still think he could order me around? Was he going to harangue me until the end?

"Good, you'd be wasting your breath," I muttered and continued to read the book.

"Smother me," he croaked.

In the gloom and nocturnal quiet of the palliative care ward my groan sounded appropriately mournful. "Ten seconds to break your word." I blinked to keep my weary eyes open. "Almost a record."

His sunken eyes stared at the ceiling. Drawn lips revealed the stumps of teeth, crooked, nicotine-stained and loose, worse now than they had been just days before. "What did you say?"

"Nothing you'd take any notice of."

He cast his frightened eyes askance at me. "It doesn't bother you, does it?" he gasped. "I'm in pain, terrible pain, that's only going to get worse according to all them so-called experts here. They won't lift a finger to help me." He gulped the hospital's sterile air. "And it's constant. I'm going to die in agony if you don't do something, son."

I believed him. His bones were trying to break through skin as smooth and dank as caul.

He fumbled with his oxygen mask and inhaled a few times before he spoke again. "Ask them specialists, Alan, if you don't believe me. Even if you don't do it for my sake, do it for your mother's. It's not fair on Carol, is it?"

"Who?"

"Making her watch me suffering with no hope of ever getting better." He returned his gaze to the ceiling like a martyred saint. "You can be cruel to me, son, but not to her. I won't stand for it."

I had no idea who Carol was, maybe the neighbour I saw by the pool on my last visit. His gaffe undermined my endeavours to remain civil. "To tell the truth, I'm not sure she'd care—Mum that is, I don't know about Carol."

Then I saw a remarkable thing, tears in his eyes, a first, surely.

The effort of emotion deflated him. He sank into his bed but barely changed its contour. "You're a weak bastard, you know that? Always have been."

An involuntary bitter chuckle seeped from me.

With his bottom lip aquiver, his chin trembling, he struggled to pull the pillow from under his head to present me with his chosen method of dispatch. I watched his farcical effort for a while from the bedside chair. He was too weak. Still, he persisted, grunting and moaning, pleading for assistance.

I ruminated on our lives together and allowed my anger to fester. Inevitably my thoughts drifted towards EC, my grief still raw and sullied with rage as I thought about the part he played in her death, dear EC, who had helped to turn my life around and gave me hope and that rare thing, love. No-one else would recognise his culpability, but I did. It was tenuous but monstrous all the same. In the peculiar stillness of the wee hours in the palliative care ward, my sense of humanity abandoned me. Suddenly I was on my feet. I snatched the pillow from him.

His mouth turned down, in a sneer or in self-pity I couldn't tell. Whatever I did, he would disapprove. I thought I heard a whimper as I pressed down hard.

22

Should I have smothered him? I've had plenty of time since to mull it over, and the answer is always the same.

23

After a moment I lifted the pillow and had the grim pleasure of seeing his terror. He sucked in air like a man desperate to live no matter what. He waved his arms around feebly and began to whimper. Why had he asked me to smother him? Perhaps he wanted me to think he was brave, that not even death scared him, counting on me to be true to form by never carrying through with his demands. He wanted to show me up one last time, to give him a reason to continue to despise me. But inadvertently I called his bluff. I saw his fear and that was enough. I put the pillow back under his head, and said, "Not yet."

Three weeks passed with him mostly insentient on opiates. Before he died, I spent long hours at night by his bedside, articulating all his failed attempts to smother me. He was unresponsive. I was calm. I was rational. And I was wrong.

He *had* smothered me. When I realised this, I was flummoxed—never smothered in the way he intended; I had resisted, managed to breath somehow, nevertheless smothered. He had set the parameters of my existence, and, like a fool, I had stayed within them. I moaned and a few unguarded tears welled. I realised I would never be free of him, even after he died.

EC would have disagreed with me. "You can be who you like," she once said, "as long as you don't let hatred rule your heart. It's a wicked master. Don't be its slave."

And, thinking of EC, my grief resurfaced. I was dead tired. My head drooped onto the bed. Her craggy smile, her generosity, her love of life filled me with remorse. I wept.

My snivelling must have aroused Tosh. I raised my head and noticed his lips move.

I thought I heard the word *sorry.*

I sat upright and leant towards him. "Say that again," I urged. "I missed it. Speak up!"

He fell into silence and I must have groaned or snivelled some more. I heard him once more, barely audible.

"What?" I repeated, almost beside myself with hope.

"Stop blubbing like a girl."

His final words.

I watched him deflate like a punctured bellows as the air seeped from him.

24

His funeral was at the Springvale Crematorium. To please my mother, I attended. Both his chicken outlet managers, my Uncle Darren and a few of his old tradie mates were at the chapel, but none the magnates he claimed to have befriended turned up. My sister gave the eulogy to spare me the indignity of speaking dishonestly or others the indignity of me speaking honestly. The service was over in twenty minutes. My pulse increased as his coffin slid through a hatch on its short journey to the furnace.

25

Two weeks after his death the government passed "assisted dying" legislation.

26

I inherited nothing but power tools from Tosh. I sold these and gave the money to an anti-battery-hen campaign. To my surprise, EC had left most of her estate to me, providing I went to Ireland and kissed the Blarney Stone for her. It seemed a facetious request. One bleak day I visited the cemetery where she was buried. Nobody else was around. I sat on a stone slab next to her grave and ruminated. A conversation we had had just before the scandal broke came back to me as I looked at the inscription, written in incomprehensible Gaelic, on her headstone. She was talking to me about her Irish ancestry for a while until I got angry with her, unfairly calling her a maudlin old soak. I expected abuse since we were both three sheets to the wind, her on stout, me drinking whiskey, but she shifted next to me and put a comradely arm around my shoulder.

"You're so bitter, my boy, why?" she sighed. "My Irishness gives my life some meaning. You don't seem to have anything. You're still young. What a waste it's going to be, this life of yours, if you let bitterness define you."

"I can't help it. I've spent my life in isolation, hating. You love Ireland. But I've got no attachments. I don't feel anything for any place. And you're about the only person I really care for. I can't stand being cynical all the time but I can't seem to do anything about it."

"If you had any humility, you could."

"That's the hardest thing," I said.

"It just requires you to recognise you're part of something greater than yourself."

I sat next to her grave and smoked a joint, knowing she would disapprove, but I was forlorn, as lonely as I had ever been.

I called out in the empty cemetery, "And what would that be?"

There was nowhere I belonged.

I looked at the trees amongst the gravestones and heard a bird calling. I watched it fly from one tree to another and down onto the ground, taking its time searching for insects, utterly indifferent to me. And I thought, it knows where it belongs, why not me?

Eventually I went to London to work on a serialised drama that needed a cynical touch. A few of my fellow screenwriters had known EC. I socialised with them and we became friends. A couple of them accompanied me across the Irish Sea to Cork, and witnessed me honouring EC's will. I learnt that kissing the Blarney Stone endowed you with the gift of the gab, particularly wit and flattery, but it wasn't going to work for me. I wasn't Irish. I hoped it would make me more eloquent with the pen instead. So, after years of screen writing, I turned my attention to prose and became a part of the tormented, wily, unsociable community of novelists.

About the Author

Graeme Sparkes was born in Launceston, Tasmania. He is the author of two travel narratives, **Beyond Tijuana** and **The Red Island**, a memoir, **You Never Met My Father**, and a novel, **Macaulay Station**. He has also worked as a teacher, itinerant labourer, taxi driver, and on the production line at a poultry slaughter-house.

www.graemesparkes.com

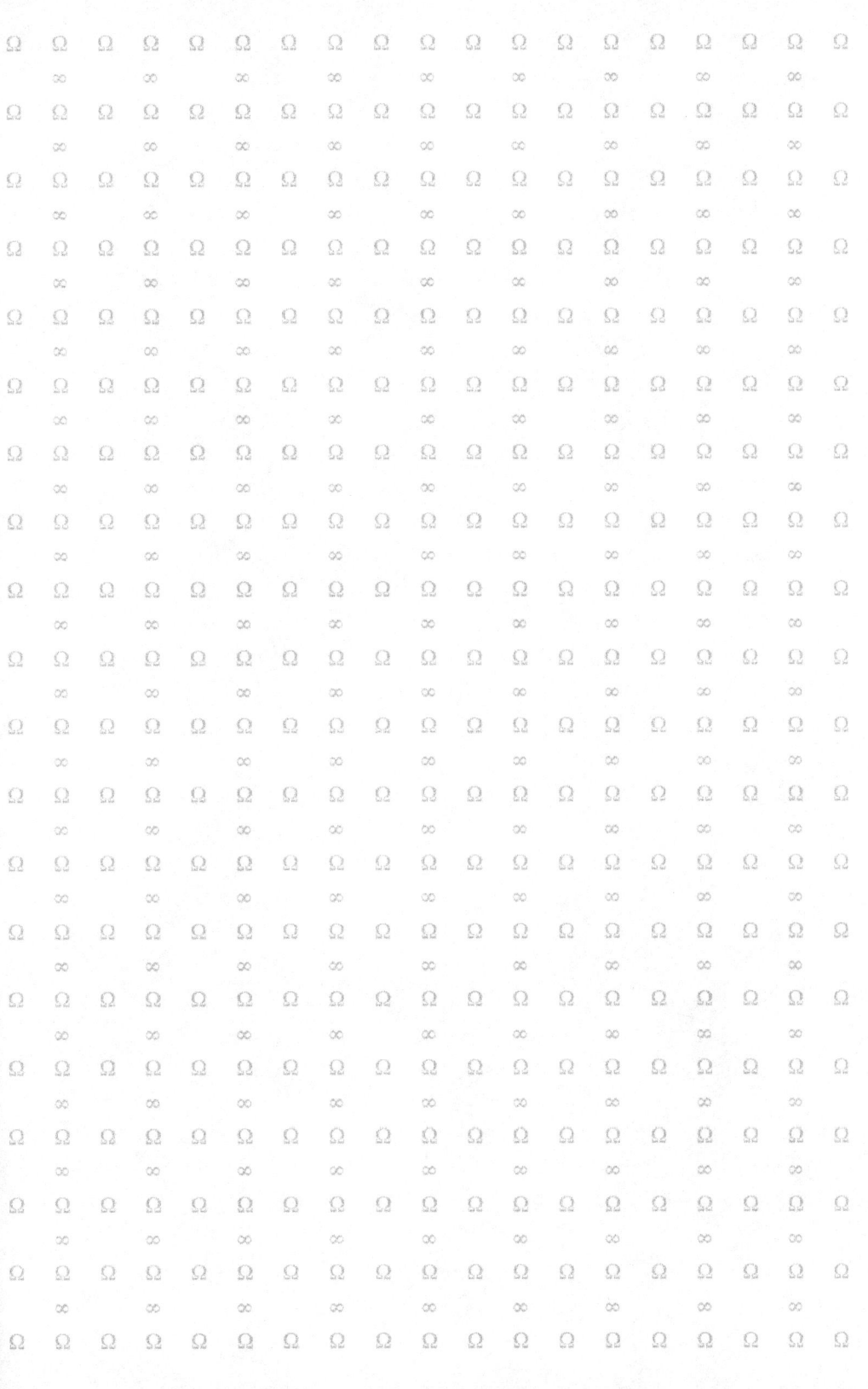

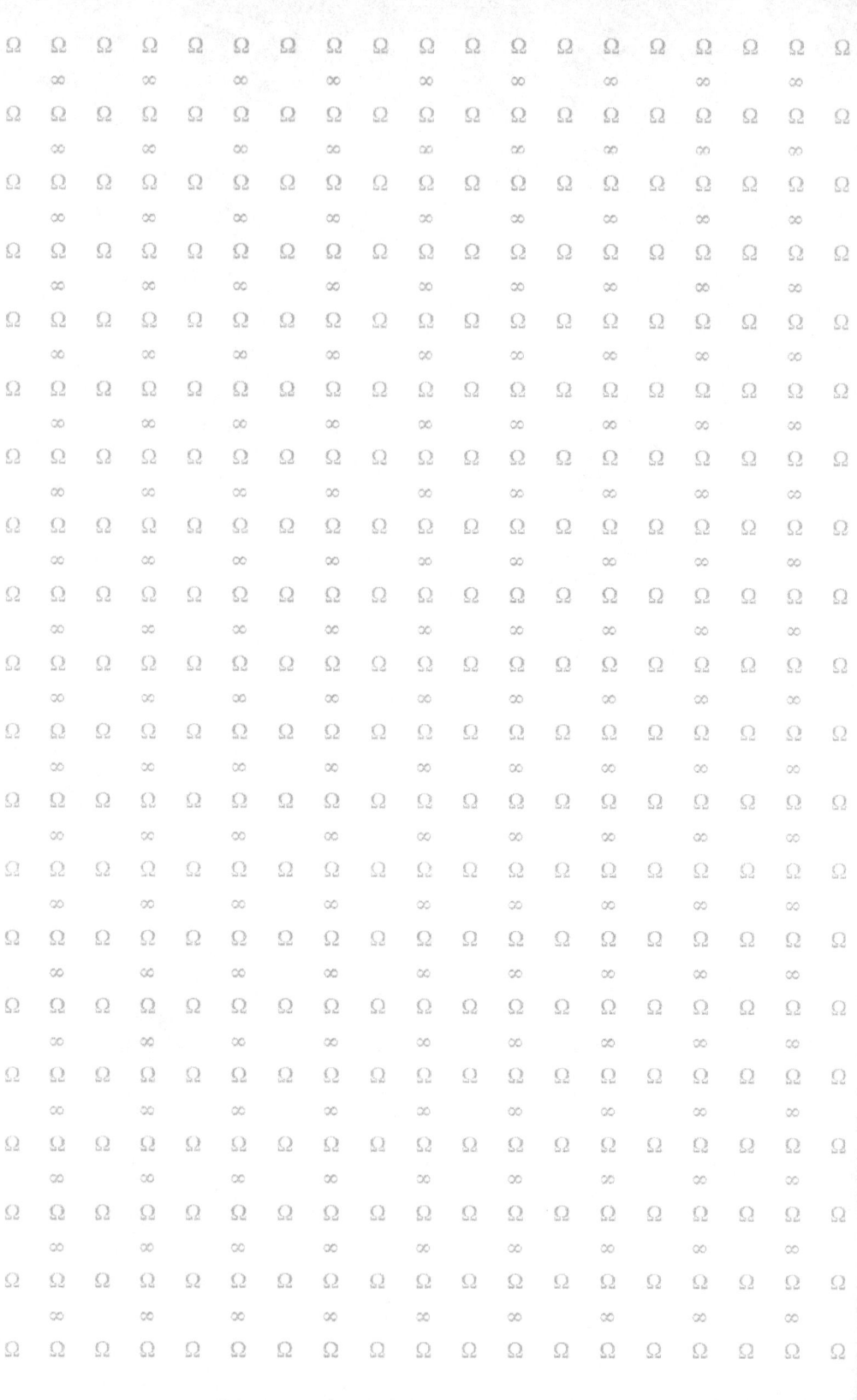

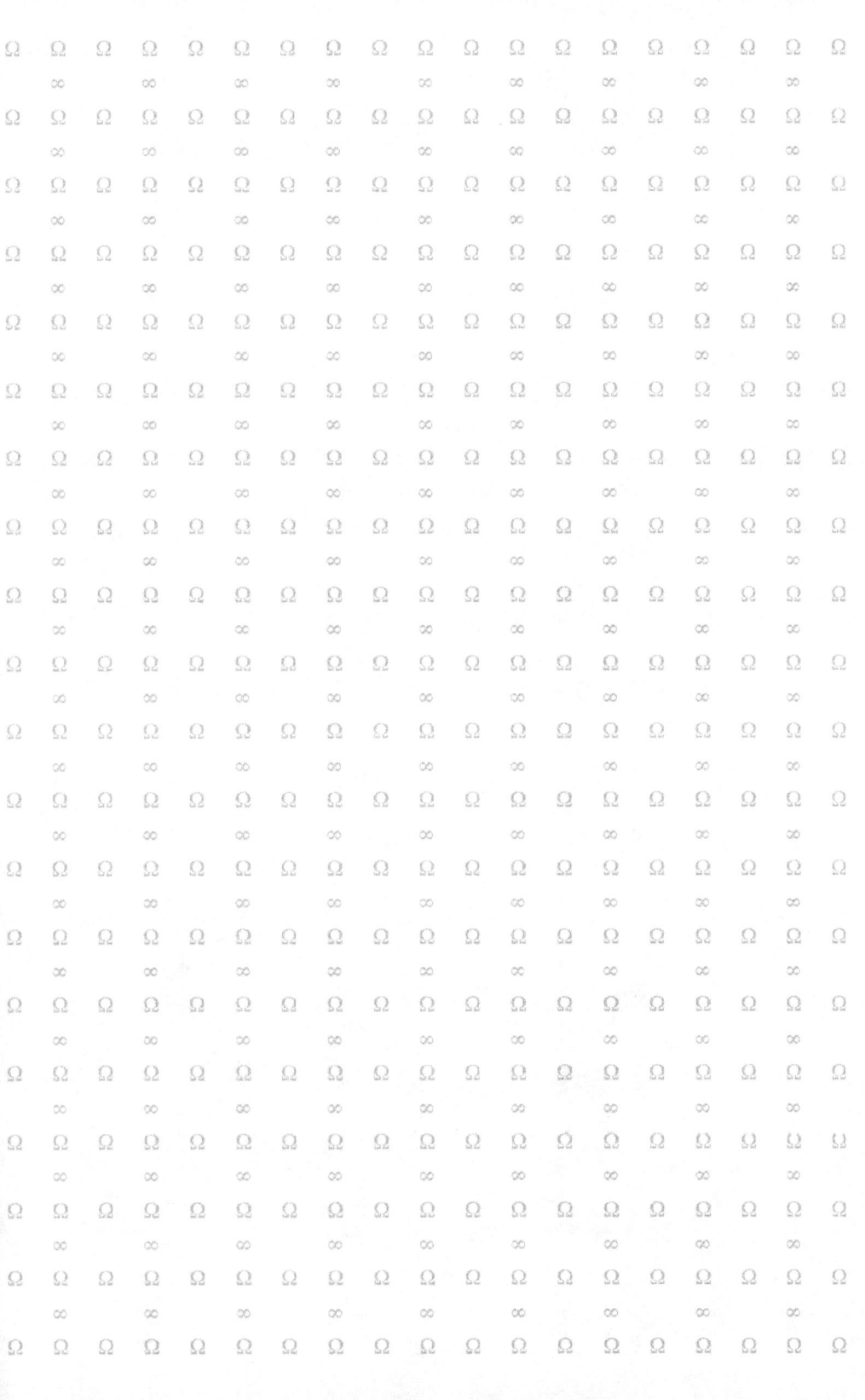